A
Mother's Hustle

Family Always First

By: Yunus Abdul Wahid

Iqra Publishing Inc

Published & Distributed by:
Iqra Publishing Inc.
157 Sunset Avenue
Atlanta, GA 30314
www.iqrapublishing.com
Edited by Chief Editor: Lori McCaskill of the IPI team.

Dedication

First, I would like to give praise to Allah for allowing me and blessing me with a way to earn my money legally while in prison after so many years. Second, I would like to dedicate this book to the following people: my mother, Charlene Lay (May Allah have mercy on her soul), R.I.P. Mama, your death still hurts after so many years. My father, Jonah Lay, for being the man of all men. Thank you Daddy and I love you so much. My babies: LaShae Sowell, Tabitha South, JaQuiesha Lay Crawford, Akilah Heard, and Jarvis Heard, and my beautiful grandkids De'Andre Miller, Aniyah Shepard, Malik South, Elijah South, David Crawford Jr., Avery Sowell, and the whole Laiboi Ent family-you know who you are. My sisters and my brothers, I love ya'll so much. Last but not least, the two women who gave me my kids and my grandkids: LaQuncia M. Heard and Erica South. To the ones who counted me out---I'm still here LOL ☺

And to Dana Shirley A.K.A. #1 Queen, thank you for your moral support, for the years you gave me and may Allah bless you, the kids, and the grandkids.

Chapter 1

"**M**ama, dats too much weed you putting in them bags. What is them you making up anyway?" Punkin asked his mama, Cha-Cha.

"I'm sacking up some nicks and some dimes, but why is you questioning me about my damn business anyway, boy?" Cha-Cha asked.

"Because you givin'em too much in these yellow envelopes for five and ten dollars," Punkin explained as he held the sacks of weed in his hand while looking at them.

"Boy, let me run my own shit! You don't know nut'n 'bout sacking up no damn weed, and put my shit down," Cha-Cha scolded him, watching him as he held the envelopes.

"Uh huh, yes I do. Much as I done watched you? And I know this too much you puttin in these yellow envelopes, Mama," Punkin explained to her.

"Now Mama, dat boy ain't got no business in here round all this stuff." Sheila explained as she put her hand on her hip, "he ain't nothin' but 10 years old goin' on 20, and plus he already knows too much as it is," Sheila commented as she shook her head side to side.

"Don't be worrying 'bout my damn baby. He ok. Shit, what do you expect when everybody 'round him is selling this shit," Cha-Cha replied?

"Come on Punkin baby, go on and sack you up some of that weed right there," Cha-Cha said while pointing to a pile of weed on the bed, "let me see what you know, since your sister wanna run her damn mouth."

"Mama," Sheila cried out, "don't be letting dat boy touch dat stuff."

"Shut the hell up! Plus, you don't tell me what the fuck to do and not do! And I wanna see if he really do know what he's doing. Just in case he has to take over the business one day." Cha-Cha went on to explain, "shit, your brother Smooth ain't trying to do nut'n but shoot up all da cocaine he can find in Atlanta with his junkie ass. Shit, he ain't done nut'n but bring hurt on this family anyway. He don't care nut'n 'bout nobody but himself, and the only thing he wanna do is get high."

Sheila couldn't do anything but just stand there shaking her head from side to side as she listened to her mama telling the truth about her oldest brother. And now here was her lil brother, who she loved so much, being made in to a man and a drug dealer at such an early age. Punkin was so smart and yet bad as hell all at the same time. Sheila realized there wasn't anything she could do about it but sit there and watch her ten-year-old brother sack up weed with their mama. At first, she was kind of angry about it, but then, she realized there was nothing she could do but go with the flow.

"Mama's right, he might have to run dis one day," Sheila thought to herself.

While she was deep in thought, she heard her mama say, "Dis damn boy really do know what he's doing."

"Let me see," Sheila said as she reached for the 3 nicks and dimes Punkin just finished sacking up.

"Dis nigga really do know what he's doing, huh? I can't wait to tell Samantha and Baby Girl about dis." Sheila replied, looking at Punkin.

"Mama, you gonna let me help you sack up all the rest of them too?" Punkin asked, while pointing to more weed he saw on the floor, in front of the closet.

"Boy, dat's 5 pounds right there."

"Sooo?!! I don't care. I still wanna help you do it," Punkin responded.

"Alright, I'll think about letting you help me when I get ready to sack it up. But right now, I want you to go check on your little brother and see what he's doing," Cha-Cha explained.

"Yes, ma'am," Punkin responded and headed downstairs.

Enos is Punkin's baby brother and the youngest child of six. They were born six years apart. Since their mama used to drink and get drunk a lot, Enos was born with Fetal Alcohol Syndrome. So as a baby, he required a lot of extra attention from the family. Punkin was his closest brother. Neither Punkin nor Enos cared for their oldest brother, Smooth. That was because of his drug habit and the way he mistreated the family. He continually put the family in danger with his drug habit. Plus, he was always stealing and lying about it.

"Enos!" Punkin called out to his lil brother from the top of the steps in their four-bedroom apartment in Carver Homes Projects.

"Huh, big bwudda?" Enos answered from downstairs.

"Whatcha doin' boy? You ain't down there gettin' into nothin' is you?" Enos yelled.

"Nuh-uh. Big bwudda, Um hawngry." Enos said while trying to climb the stairs.

"Okay, stay right there. Here I come. And what you want to eat?" Punkin asked. As he walked downstairs, he could hear Sheila on the phone with their sister, Samantha.

Sheila was telling Samantha about him sacking up his first sack of weed. Now with a big smile on his face, Punkin thought, "*Yep, and one day I'll have all that plus much more and be real rich with a lot of money.*"

As he got to the bottom of the stairs, he took Enos's hand and said, "Come on lil bruh, let's go fix you something to eat."

"O-tay big bwudda, luh ou," Enos told him.

"I love you too lil bruh. What you wanna eat 'til Mama finish handling her business and come cook us something?" Punkin asked.

"Uhmmm, dem bickles and hot dawse. What ou gon' eat?" Enos asked.

"I dunno. I might fix me a couple of grilled cheese sandwiches. Why? You want one too?" Punkin inquired.

Enos just looked at his big brother with a big smile on his face. He shook his head up and down to tell his big brother, "YES!" Punkin went to the fridge and grabbed a long brown box that had a big block of what everyone referred to as "government cheese". After he put that on the counter, he turned around and grabbed the butter. Punkin gave the butter to Enos to hold while he pulled a chair from the kitchen table over to the fridge. Standing on the chair, he grabbed the loaf of Colonial bread from the top of the fridge. He put the bread, butter, and cheese on the counter and went to get the big black skillet from under the kitchen sink. After rinsing out the skillet, he put it on the stove. He then tore off a piece of the brown paper bag that was in the corner and rolled it up. He stuck it inside the gas stove until it caught fire from the pilot light. He then turned on the front left eye on the stovetop and lit the eye for the skillet.

Chapter 2

"Boy, what the hell is y'all two bad-asses down there doing in my damn kitchen," their mama, Cha-Cha, screamed from the top of the steps.

"Cooking me and my lil brutha some'n to eat, mama. He told me he was hungry," Punkin yelled back from the kitchen.

"Who in the hell told you to cook anything down there in MY damn kitchen, huh? And anyway, what do you call yourself down there cooking? You better not burn my motherfuckin' apartment down," she yelled.

"Yes, ma'am. I'm cooking us some grilled cheese sandwiches. You know when my lil brutha told me he was hungry, I had to feed him Mama, "Punkin explained.

"Big bwudda, is we gon' git in twouble?" Enos asked, looking up at Punkin with fear in his eyes, because he didn't want to get a whoopin.

"Naw, we ain't gonna get in no trouble," Punkin answered as he hugged Enos to make his lil brutha feel better.

"You better make sure you clean up whatever the fuck you fucked up in that kitchen, because I still gotta cook before Droup get his ass home from work. You know how his drunk ass is, and I ain't trying to hear his damn mouth 'bout me not having his food ready. Matter of fact, while you're down there, go on ahead and take out that chicken that's in the freezer, and run some cold water on it for dinner," Cha-Cha instructed Punkin.

Droup is Punkin's and Enos's real daddy, but as far as all six of them were concerned, he was daddy to all of them. When Cha-Cha and Droup first met, Cha-Cha already had four kids of her own. Their father was nowhere to be found, therefore, not in their lives at all. So as any real man would do when he got with a woman whom had kids, he raised all six of them as if they were his own. He never mistreated any of them. He loved them all and would do anything he could to make sure they were happy.

Even though Droup liked to drink his liquor and beer 'til he got drunk, he was a very hard-working man and a damn good husband and father to his kids. No matter how cold it was, how sick he was, or how far he had to walk, he made sure he went to work five days a week; sometimes, he went all seven. He wouldn't even cash his check before coming home. Rather he would come home and pick up Cha-

Cha, and they would go together, cash it, then he would allow her to manage all the money. He would make sure that he gave her nearly his whole check to make sure all the bills in the apartment were paid, food was in the apartment, and that his kids were taken care of. He would only keep 50 dollars for himself to carry him to the next Friday. As long as he had something to drink when he got off work and a home-cooked meal when he got home, he was straight.

"Yes, ma'am," Punkin said as he went to the fridge and opened the top where the chicken was. He grabbed a bag of leg quarters and placed them in the sink. He turned on the cold water to thaw the chicken.

"Come on lil bruh, let's get ready to eat. Go on and sit at the table while I grab our sandwiches outta the skillet," Punkin said, as he and grabbed some plates for them.

Enos took off running to the kitchen table, pulled out a chair, jumped up in it, and turned around while standing in the chair. He was waiting on his grilled cheese sandwich and pickles with hot sauce.

"Sit down, Enos, before you fall and hurt yourself," Punkin warned.

"I ain' gonna fall big bwudda," Enos fired back

"A'ight now, if you fall your butt outta that chair, you better not start no crying," Punkin explained.

"Awight. Big bwudda, you gon' make us sum Koo-aid?" Enos asked.

"Yeah, I will fix us some Kool-Aid, but you gotta sit down in your chair first."

"O-tay," Enos replied as he turned around and sat down.

Punkin grabbed two small plates, two glasses, and then got a butter knife and a spatula from the drawer. He fumbled as he used the spatula to turn the grilled cheese sandwiches to cook evenly on both sides. After he scooped the third sandwich from the skillet, he turned off the eye and put the hot skillet in the sink and ran cold water on it while it sizzled and smoked up the kitchen.

He cut one of the three grilled cheese sandwiches in half, so he could share it with his brother, so they both had one and a half sandwiches. Then he put pickles and hot sauce on Enos's plate. He set the plates on the table and then went and got a pitcher of watermelon Kool-Aid from the fridge and poured them each a glass of it. He put the pitcher of Kool-Aid back in the fridge and grabbed their glasses and brought them to the table. He sat down, and they began to eat. As soon as they had taken a bite, they heard *knock, knock, knock, knock, knock* at the door.

"Dumboly at da doe big bwudda," Enos said, turning his body in the direction of the knock on the door.

"I know. Stay right there while I go get Mama." Punkin replied.

"Who is it?" They both heard Sheila inquire before Punkin got a chance to get out of the kitchen.

"Girl, open up this damn door!" They heard their other big sister, Baby Girl, say from the other side of the door.

"Big sista, that's Baby Girl at the door." Punkin said as he met Sheila at the entrance to the kitchen, which was next to the front door. Sheila opened the front door to let her little sister, Baby Girl, in. Baby Girl stepped inside wearing some Adidas shorts and an Adidas shirt with a pair of green and white Stan Smith Adidas tennis shoes. She also wore a pair of big, gold, hoop earrings with a diamond stud in the hole next to the hoop. Her hair was cut short in a style that showed she was feeling fresh. Sheila stood looking at her little sister in admiration.

"Where my mama at? And why is you standing there wit yo' stank ass lookin' at me like that?" Baby Girl asked with a smile on her face.

"She's upstairs, and who in the hell did your red ass trick to dress you all up and shit? And don't you sit there and tell me nobody, cuz your red ass is too dang jazzy for you to sit up here and try to even think about telling me a lie," Sheila said with a smile on her face as she joked with her baby sister.

"Bitch, go to hell. I ain't tricked no-damn-body. Me and one of my niggas just came back from shopping downtown. He hit a big ass lick last night, so you know I had to put this pussy on him like I hadn't fucked in a hundred damn months," Baby Girl spit back while moving her head from side to side as she laughed.

"Bitch, you so damn stupid. And which one, hell, you got so many mens to choose from? Naw forget that, let me tell you 'bout this lil brutha of yours standing here with his bad ass," Sheila replied.

"What the hell his grown ass done did now?" Baby Girl asked while looking at her little brother, who was just standing there with a smile on his face. Punkin waited for Sheila to tell Baby Girl the news of him sacking up his first bags of weed. Right as Sheila was about to tell the story, Enos came running in the room and jumped into Baby Girl's arms.

"Heeeyyyyy big susta," Enos yelled jumping in her arms.

"Hey baby! What you been eating boy?" Baby Girl asked as she picked him up and hugged.

"My big bwudda, Punkin, cook us dum gwill teeee dammiches; ou wan' dum?" Enos asked.

"Naw, baby. I'm ok. I just finished eating. Now what was you finna say 'bout this bad ass right here?" Baby Girl asked while moving Enos to her hip.

"Girl, do you know Mama let this lil fucka sack up some damn weed with her not too long ago," Sheila told her.

"No the hell she didn't. What the fuck is wrong with Mama, has she lost her damn mind? Why in the hell didn't you beat his lil ass?" Baby Girl inquired.

"Who?! Shiiit, you know how Mama is about that damn boy. You know can't nobody touch him without getting cursed out. She cursed me out when I tried to say somethin' about it," Sheila responded.

"That's why his lil ass is so damn grown and bad as hell now, 'cause can't nobody whoop'm. What the hell you standing there smiling at me for?! You know you ain't got no damn business putting your hands on that shit. I oughta beat yo' ass myself," Baby Girl told him.

Just as Baby Girl was talking, their mama walked around the corner into the kitchen after standing there listening to them.

"Hell naw, I ain't lost my fucking mind, and you of all people ain't gonna put your fucking hands on him. Just like I told Sheila's ass, shit, all of us sell this shit right in front of him every damn day. If he go'n do it, I rather it be me teachin' him than the punk ass niggas in these streets. Shit, somebody's go'n have to take over what I am trying to build one day when I'm tired. And it damn sure can't be y'all or that damn no-good Smooth," Cha-Cha explained.

"Mama, you know that boy is too damn young to be messin' with that stuff," Baby Girl explained with Enos on her hip as she pointed at Punkin with her free hand.

At that point Sheila told them to stop it and told Baby Girl to come on upstairs with her, because no matter what any of them had to say to their mama, it wasn't going to do any good, because her mind was already made up.

"Come on girl, let's go on upstairs," Sheila said to Baby Girl.

"Yeah, you better get that lil red-ass bitch before I kill her ass. Fuck she think she is anyway, comin' in my damn apartment running her mouth?" Cha-Cha asked.

Baby Girl was just about to say something when Sheila put her hand over her mouth to keep her quiet.

"Just shut up, Baby Girl, please. Don't say nothin' back, because you know how she is. So come on, let's just go on upstairs," Sheila begged wisely.

Baby Girl was about to buck up to her mama, but what Sheila said made her think twice, and she went upstairs with her.

"I know that's right. You better take her mother-fucking ass upstairs if you know what's good for her ass," Cha-Cha yelled after them.

"Mama, leave the girl alone now. She gone upstairs, "Sheila replied.

Baby Girl and her mama rarely got along, because they were so much alike. The only real difference between the two was their mama had brown skin, whereas Baby Girl's skin had a reddish tint to it. But as far as height, weight, size, attitude, and facial features, they were exactly the same. They acted so much alike that they couldn't stand each other, yet they loved each other to death at the same time.

"Punkin come here! I thought I told you to clean up this dam mess when you were finished fuckin' it up." Cha-Cha scolded him.

"Oh, yes ma'am, I ain't forgot. I'ma do it right now." said Punkin.

"Alright now, don't let me have to got on yo ass, too." warned Cha-Cha.

"I got this mama," Punkin said as he and Enos finished eating, and started cleaning the kitchen right away.

Chapter 3

Punkin walked outside right after he finished cleaning the kitchen, but Enos stayed inside.

"I sure wish Daddy was here so he could beat that boy's damn ass for even having that thought in his head, "Baby Girl said.

"Girl, you might as well let that shit go. 'Cause you know Daddy is just going to sit there and look crazy. You know he ain't gonna say shit to Mama, either. Hell, I can't even get Samantha to get on Mama, and we both know she's the only one who can say something and not get cursed out," Sheila said.

"What she say?" Baby Girl inquired.

"Nothing. Hell, she just said what can anybody do about it? Mama is going to be mama. She raised all four of us and look at us… So, what else should we expect? He's her favorite of all of us, besides Enos, so she's gonna give him da game," Sheila explained.

"Well, if that lil fucker ever make it big, he better make sure he take care of me, like I used to do his little shitty ass.

Had me wiping all that shit off his ass when he was a baby," Baby Girl complained.

"Girl, you so damn stupid," Sheila joked with her big sister.

"Stupid, my ass. I'm dead ass serious," Baby Girl emphasized. They both started laughing.

BANG! BANG! BANG! BANG!

Punkin was curious as to where the shots were coming from and lingered outside.

"Punkin! Get yo' ass in this house! I know you heard them damn gunshots!" Cha-Cha said.

"Mama, them shots is coming from behind the school. I'm alright," Punkin said standing next to the tree and he was about to climb.

"I don't give a fuck where they coming from! Get your damn ass in here right now!" Cha-Cha yelled.

Right at that moment, Punkin saw a guy running from behind the school full speed with blood all over him and his clothes. He was clutching his stomach as he ran across the Price High School parking lot. He finally made it across the street and ran past Punkin, and he saw sweat on the dude's face and fear in his eyes. The guy had on a blue T-shirt, blue and white shorts, and all the way to his knees, they were covered in blood. Punkin felt like he was in a movie for the first time in his life, and strangely enough, he liked it. As he watched, he noticed the man's left eye was swollen, and his lips were bleeding. The man made it across Jenkins street right into Punkin's neighbors' yard (Mama Dear, Lil Net, and Mr. and Mrs. King's). The man fell and died right next to a tire that was being used as a flower pot.

Once the man fell, Punkin looked back over to the school and saw no one else coming from behind the school after him. That's when Punkin heard his mama scream out to his sisters, Sheila and Baby Girl, who were still in the apartment, "Call the ambulance before he dies."

At that time, Punkin could only guess that one of them went and called. His only concern was getting across the street to see the wounded guy laying in the yard.

Punkin saw many of the neighbors coming outside to go over and stand around the man. That's when he finally made his way over to the crowd hovering over him looking down at his body. Right then he noticed the man had been shot about five times. Once in the chest, two times in the stomach, and twice in his left leg. It was already too late; This poor guy was dead for sure.

There was blood coming out of his mouth, either from his busted lip, or his dying experience. He also had blood coming out of the other five holes in his body. Punkin couldn't see how in the hell he made it from behind that school, considering how many times he had been shot. But it's true what they say: a person will do the most amazing shit out of fear and when adrenaline kicks in with their life on the line.

At that very moment, something inside of Punkin changed, taking a turn for the worse. All in one day and at the tender age of 10, his whole life had changed. Earlier in the day he was sacking up his first sack of weed with his mama. Now there he was standing over his first dead body just a few hours later. Punkin had a cold and callously sinister demeanor about him that spoke volumes about his inner self: a haunting smile on his face, fire in his eyes, and an eerie calmness about him. He knew at that moment, he was ready to become his own boss. He knew he would be the one to set the example that needed to be set and wouldn't take shit from nobody, period.

Punkin didn't notice peripherally out of the corner of his left eye that one of the neighbors was tapping his mama on the shoulder, pointing at him. He was so lost in his own little trance, he never even noticed his mama standing by him. But when she looked and saw what he was doing, she turned and grabbed Punkin by his arm and yelled at him.

"Boy, what the fuck is wrong with you? Why in the hell you got that stupid ass smile on your face? Have you lost your damn mind? Get your ass in the damn house, right now!" Cha-Cha scolded Punkin.

Punkin stormed off heading back to their apartment thinking to himself, "That neighbor is one snitching ass bitch; somebody needs to kill her ass." But instead of going inside like his mama said, he just sat on the front porch steps, looking at the crowd across the street.

As Punkin was sitting there, he noticed the Doppler effect of emergency vehicles approaching, they were getting closer and closer as the sirens got louder and louder. A few seconds later, he saw two police cars pulling up to where the crowd was across the street. The officers then got out of their cars making people back up from around the dead body. One of the officers went back to his police car, opened the trunk, and grabbed a big yellow role of tape with black words on it, POLICE LINE DO NOT CROSS. He commanded the crowd not to cross the taped off crime scene.

The officer went back to the body where he and another officer started putting up the yellow tape. While they were doing that, the other two officers were asking people in the crowd questions. A few moments later, an ambulance pulled up with two paramedics. They got out and tried to work on the dead man's body. Punkin could only guess that they were trying to see if the man could be saved, but Punkin knew he was dead from standing over him. After the paramedics realized they could not save him, they went back to the ambulance and grabbed the stretcher and a black bag. When the paramedics went back to the body, one of them got down on one knee and unzipped the black body bag. He and his partner put the body in the bag, scooped it up, put him in the back of the ambulance, and drove off.

Punkin saw his mama and a couple of the neighbors standing around talking for a while after the police and ambulance left, then all of them headed back to their apartments looking sad, shaking their heads in disbelief. But not all of them went back to their apartments, a couple of them turned and headed towards Punkin's apartment with his mama. When they got into their front yard, Punkin could hear one of them asking his mama if she had some weed for sale.

"That's that snitchin ass neighbor. I can't wait 'til I'm old enough to shoot her," Punkin thought to himself.

"Punkin!" Cha-Cha yelled, as she was coming toward the porch where Punkin was sitting.

"Yes, ma'am?"

"Go in the house and go upstairs. Get me my purple Crown Royal bag with them sacks of weed in it. It should be on my night stand, right next to my bed," Cha-Cha told him.

"Yes, ma'am!" Punkin replied.

As Punkin headed up the stairs to get the weed for his mama, he could hear her telling the neighbors about some new stuff she was about to get in called 'Tie Stick.' So, Punkin, being nosy after hearing this, stopped instantly on the steps to soak up game about what she was saying. She was telling them it was going to cost $10 to get one joint of this weed that she had coming in.

One of their neighbors said, "$10 for a joint? What the fuck typa weed is this shit? It better make me forget who the fuck I am and then keep me high so damn long that I start praying to God to stop the high." At that point they all started laughing.

Punkin then went on up the rest of the steps to get the bag for mama, and just like he figured, as soon as he got to the bag, Cha-Cha yelled out his name. So, he took off running back down the steps to hurry to give her the bag.

"What the fuck took you so long up them steps, boy? You better not have been up there fucking with my shit!" Cha-Cha warned.

"I ain't been up there doing nothing, mama!" Punkin tried to explain.

"You better not have," Cha-Cha warned, "now go on in there and see if that chicken is ready, so I can start cooking before your daddy gets home."

"Yes, ma'am" Punkin replied.

Punkin went into the kitchen like his mama told him to. He checked on the chicken that was in the sink with cold water still running on it. He hollered out of the kitchen and told his mama that it was ready while she stayed in the living room talking to their neighbors a little while longer. They smoked a couple of joints and then left, heading for their own apartments.

As soon as Cha-Cha came back in the kitchen, Punkin asked her, "Mama, what is Tie Stick?"

"How in the hell do you know about Tie Stick?" she asked, looking at him suspiciously and continued, "so that is what took you so damn long to get my bag. You had your little ass on them steps listening, didn't you?"

"Yes ma'am."

"I knew you was lying," Cha-Cha's intuition prevailed, "why you told me nothin' when I asked what you was doing up there that took you so long?"

"Because I don't like that lady. She got me in trouble for nothing," Punkin tried to explain.

"Boy, you was standing up there looking at a dead man with a smile on your face! Shit! Matter of fact, what was you smilin' at?

"I don't know; for some reason, I like what I saw in the man," Punkin said.

"What you mean you liked it?! What the fuck is wrong witchoo boy, is you crazy?" Cha-Cha asked.

"No," Punkin said with barely a whisper as he looked down at the floor. He knew when his mama got like this she did not play, not even with him.

"No, what? I done told you about that shit! And hold your head up!" Cha-Cha ordered.

"No ma'am," Punkin replied.

"LOOK Punkin, I DON'T WANTCHOO TO END UP IN PRISON LOCKED AWAY FOR THE REST OF YOUR LIFE. DO YOU HEAR ME?! BECAUSE IT IS NOT OK TO KILL PEOPLE!" Cha-Cha yelled at Punkin.

Cha-Cha was now much calmer and had a seriousness in her eyes as she held Punkin's chin up forcing him to look her in her eyes.

"But Mama, I can't let no nigga kill me either. Everybody always told me someone else looks better laying there dead than I do. Plus, I would rather be judged by 12 than carried by 6," Punkin explained.

"Boy, who in the hell been telling you dis shit?" Cha-Cha asked, with a confused look on her face.

At that point, Punkin knew that when he told her that, it was his two older brothers, Nathan and Charlie, and that they would be in trouble as soon as she saw them. But he couldn't lie either.

"My big brothers, Nathan and Charlie," he told her.

Nathan was a hustler whom mama used to sell weed to. Out of nowhere, he became part of the family. All of the family loved him to death and respected him just as if he was born from their mother's womb. He was also the big brother Punkin never had. Punkin guessed that the reason was because Nathan knew his real big brother was strung out on drugs real bad. The other thing Punkin loved about him was he never took any disrespect unless it was coming from their mama since she was 'Head Lady In Charge.'

Charlie, on the other hand, was Punkin's cousin, but he called him his big brother. He was always loaded with a bunch of money, plus, he was always looking fresh. Another thing was that he was putting Punkin up on all type of game. Whether it was the streets or females, he made sure Punkin knew what he needed to know to survive out in the world.

"I'm going to curse both of they asses out when they get home," Cha-Cha said as she stood at the kitchen sink pulling the chicken apart.

"Is they lying to me, Mama?" Punkin asked.

"No, they ain't telling you a lie, but I just don't want you thinking it's OK to go around killing people, Punkin," Cha-Cha explained.

"You got people out here killing every day, and I can't end up like that dude out there dead in the neighbor's front yard," Punkin tried explaining, but Cha-Cha wouldn't hear any of it.

"Them fuckers is fucking up your head and making you crazy just like them. Even though I know you can't be soft growing up in these projects, but you don't have to be all hard and heartless either," Cha-Cha said as she looked at Punkin.

Cha-Cha was trying to talk some sense into Punkin, but he wasn't trying to hear what she had to say. He felt like he had to get his respect by any means necessary when he got older. He would not tolerate disrespect from anyone but his daddy and her. His mind was made up at 10 years old.

Chapter 4

Before the screen door even opened, Punkin could hear Charlie and Nathan coming up the steps laughing and talking. Even before they entered the apartment, as soon as they had stepped inside the front door, they were met by Punkin's mama, and she snapped right off the bat.

"What the fuck have y'all been tellin my damn baby? And don't look like y'all don't know what the fuck I'm talking about!" Cha-Cha snapped at Nathan and Charlie, as they stood in the entryway looking confused.

They both just stood there looking at each other with a "What the fuck is going on?" look on their faces.

"Wassup shawty? What we done did? You just snapped at us for no reason. We don't know whatchu talkin' about," Charlie said, looking at Cha-Cha for answers.

"I ain't snapped yet! And y'all damn well know what the fuck I'm talkin' 'bout. Nathan get that stupid-ass look off your face right damn now!" Cha-Cha raged.

"Mama, what the hell have we done? Please let us know!" Nathan said, meek and humble.

"Somebody got shot behind the school and ran from back there. He died in Mama Dear and them's yard."

"OK and what? We didn't do it, baby." Nathan said, with a smile on his face.

"Shut your damn mouth and listen! If you wasn't running your damn mouth so much, you'd know why in the hell I'm pissed the fuck off!" Cha-Cha said while pointing the same kitchen knife she had been using to cut the chicken with at Nathan.

"Alright now Nathan, you know how shawty is when she gets mad, and I ain't about to get cut for your ass either," Charlie said.

"Don't tell his ass nothin', I'ma cut from asshole to appetite," their mama said.

"Ok, baby. You right," Nathan said holding his hands up in the air, "but still… What have we done to you?" Nathan asked.

"It ain't me y'all done it to, it's y'all damn lil brother standing right here," Cha-Cha explained looking from Nathan to Charlie and back again.

"We ain't did nothing to him. Boy, what the hell have you done told Mama?" Charlie said while they both looked at Punkin with anger in their eyes.

"Nothin'" Punkin said.

"Today when that damn man got shot and ran past Punkin… Punkin just stood there and watched him. But then when he collapsed and died across the street in their yard, then his lil ass went over there and was standing over the man--- smiling. There ain't shit to smile about when somebody gets shot dead. He had that same damn smile you be havin' on your face, Nathan. This boy is taking up all y'all's crazy-ass habits," Cha-Cha snapped at them.

"Ok, that might be the truth, but what we still don't see is what we got to do with any of dis Mama?" Charlie asked, still not understanding.

"It's coming from all dis shit that y'all be telling him about how 'someone else look better laying down there dead than he do,' and all that shit about 'rather be judged by 12 than carried by 6.' And who knows what the fuck else y'all been telling my baby," Cha-Cha explained.

By this time Nathan spoke up, trying to talk some sense into their mama.

"Look mama, dis here is my lil nigga and my lil brotha, and yeah, I told him all of that. I don't regret one word of it

29

neither. Damn right I'd rather see another nigga laying down there dead with flowers growing on his bitch-ass than to see my little brother down there. Mama, we all know these streets is nothing but a war zone. I'll train him to kill every nigga he sees and that tries him before I let my little brother be soft and get fucked over by any of these pussy-ass niggas," Nathan said.

"But this damn boy is just 10 years old, Nathan, and he ain't in them damn streets yet either," Cha-Cha tried to explain.

"You're right, he ain't yet, but just take a look at how much he knows already, and what all he done seen at his age. Hell, Mama, we smoke and drink in front of him, and we sack up pounds of weed in front of him. Shit, he be with Charlie so much, ain't no telling what else he done seen and learned out there in them streets," Nathan said.

"Shiiit Shawty, you know Nathan is right. We know you love dis lil nigga, but sidd shawty, you don't think we love him too? He's our little brother so you know damn well we'll kill a brick and put a rock in the hospital 'bout him," Charlie explained.

As Punkin stood there and watched Nathan and Charlie talking to his mama, he noticed her anger was starting to cool down 'cause it was all starting to make sense to her. Much as she hated to admit it... They were right. Although she would never admit it to them because of her position and pride, but her body language said it all.

"See Mama, what I tell you?! Now you see how I felt this morning when you was letting him sack up that weed with you, and you cursed me out for saying something about it," Sheila said.

"Hell, she just cursed me out not too long ago right here in this very spot," Baby Girl said waving her hand around to indicate where they were standing.

"Where the fuck y'all two come from any way? Is y'all eavesdropping on us?" Cha-Cha asked Sheila and Baby Girl.

"Eavesdropping? Come on, Mama. Let's be real. We saw them coming in the front yard, and we started coming down the steps, and that's when we heard you snappin at them about your little grown-ass baby," Baby Girl said.

"Go to hell. And you damn right, I'm being real. I don't trust yo red-ass." Cha-Cha replied.

"Hold on! Hold on! Hold on!" Nathan said waving his hands in the air to get everyone's attention. "You just snapped on me and Charlie for giving him the motto of staying alive, but you got him sacking up weed? Come on Mama, let's be serious," Nathan said.

"Um hmm, yep," Baby Girl said.

"I'ma 'umm hmm yep' yo' ass, just keep on with your damn smart-ass remarks. And hell yeah, I'm serious as a heart attack. Teaching him how to hustle is way different from teaching him how to be a killa," Cha-Cha replied, hoping they understood the difference.

"But shawty, it all goes hand in hand," Charlie said.

"It sho nuff do Mama," Sheila added in.

"And to think I was starting to feel bad about it, now I gotta sho nuff turn up the volume and learn him what the hell is going on outthere in the streets. 'Cause ain't no doubt in my mind, this little nigga is going to sell him some dope," Nathan explained.

"Anyway, what the hell y'all call yourselves doing teaming up on me? All y'all can go to hell!" Cha-Cha said looking at each of them in turn, "matter of fact, all y'all go on and get the hell out of my face! I don't want to hear no more of this shit. Plus, I gotta start cooking before y'all daddy get home."

"Don't you get mad at us for telling you the truth. It is what it is, and right now the truth is what it is," Sheila told her mama.

"Sheila's right, Mama, but go ahead and get that drunk-ass man's food ready, because we all know he don't play, and I ain't standin' in the way. He ain't going to choke me to damn

32

death with that damn hand of his just because his food ain't ready," Nathan said. He cuffed three of his fingers, just leaving his pinky and thumb showing, indicating their daddy's hand that only has two fingers on it. They all started laughing.

Chapter 5

"P
unkin," Cha-Cha said as she turned to him. "Ma'am?" Punkin responded.

"Go outside and play so I can talk to your sisters and your brothers. You've heard enough as it is. Take Enos witchu. Matter of fact, where is my baby at anyway?" Cha-Cha asked.

"He's upstairs sleep in Sheila bed," Baby Girl said.

"Why I gotta go outside and play? I wanna stay in here with y'all," Punkin said.

Soon as Punkin opened his mouth and said that, his big brother, Nathan, grabbed him by the collar of his shirt and told him, "Nigga, when Mama tell you to do something, you do it. You hear me? Your lil ass ain't grown, so you don't question her! Even if you was grown, you still don't question her. Now get your ass outside and play like she said… You better not leave out that front yard. Now go on," he said while slapping Punkin upside his head.

As soon as Punkin was outside, Cha-Cha led the rest of them to the kitchen table, where they all sat down. With a look of seriousness and concern on her face, Cha-Cha started explaining what was about to happen.

"Look, all y'all know dat's my baby, and I admit that I might do some things dat's not right or motherly at times when it comes to dealing wit Punkin. But in my eyes, I'm doing what's best for him and not y'all. I already done raised y'all and still raising y'all as far as I'm concerned. And when it comes down to it, who else do I have here dat I'ma be able to rely on to run dis shit when I'm old and gray?" Cha-Cha asked the group.

Cha-Cha looked at Sheila, "Sheila, you have your own family to raise now, and DeWayne is driving your ass fucking crazy. So that alone goes to show you have your own problems, plus you're too scared to hustle when it comes down to it," Cha-Cha said as Sheila looked away, knowing she was right.

She then turned her attention to Baby Girl.

"And you, Baby Girl, with your red-ass, you is too damn sneaky and conniving to be trusted. You'll tell a lie before God gets the damn news. I know you're my child, but you and me, we like oil and water, we just don't mix," Cha-Cha said as Baby Girl's face turned dark with anger.

Cha-Cha then turned to look at Nathan.

"Nathan, even though you ain't my child, I've raised you just like you're one of my own. So, I know you better than you know yourself, and your problem is you love to put your dick in every damn female you see. You'll let a hoe trick you outta your whole damn lifesavings, 'cause all you care about is a nut and a big butt. Plus, you're too damn hot-headed... Just like what you're trying to turn my damn baby into," she layed out as Nathan took a moment to think about what she said.

Then she turned her attention to Charlie.

"And finally Charlie, you on the other hand, I could see you running dis, but your only problem is that you love to smoke those geek joints, rob, steal cars for no reason when you got enough money to buy ten of them. So, you not ready to run dis and probably never will be. I don't want to even mention dat fucking brother of y'all's, Smooth, 'cause we all know I most definitely won't and can't trust him. Now y'all's sista, Samantha, on the other hand, is my brains and my advisor in the whole situation, plus she is the only one who keeps her head on her shoulders, and she could run it. But I'm not going to let her--- she got a bigger calling in life," Cha-Cha explained.

"I agree with you on that, but we all know dat Samantha is the most spoiled out of all of us, besides Enos and Punkin," Nathan said.

"Shut your damn mouth boy... I ain't playing witchu right now. Plus, you and Charlie is being put ova my baby. He don't hardly listen to anybody but y'all. Especially you Nathan. I don't know what you is doing to him, but I know one thang... You better make him the best at whateva you teaching him. And if he is going to be a heartless, ruthless mother-fucker, he better be able to think also. Dat really just hurt me to say that to y'all about my baby. It's like I'm losing my mind, but hell at least I know that someone who truly loves him will be helping him. I'm grooming him already to be a hustler, because I can see it in him already. Today when I let him sack up dat weed with me, it showed me he's a fast learner. And now it's up to you two to finish grooming him as far as the streets is concerned. I'ma finish teaching him the ropes on my end of him hustling. Do not make me regret my decision, because if I do---y'all is fucking dead meat," Cha-Cha explained while staring at Nathan and Charlie.

"Who's dead?" Sheila asked.

"Charlie and Nathan, dat's who. You act like you got a problem with it," Cha-Cha said while continuing to cut up the chicken for dinner.

"Well I guess both of y'all's asses heard that," she said while pointing her finger at Nathan and Charlie, who just stood there smiling at their sister. Baby Girl, on the other hand, just stood there the whole time not saying a word, because she knew one word could turn her mother's wrath straight on her. She did have that sneaky look in her eyes that said, "I'll make you pay for this one-day Mama," but little did she know that day would never come, because her mama was always 5 steps ahead of her.

"What do me and Baby Girl have to do with this conversation? Because the whole time you just been talking to these two niggas," Sheila asked.

"I wanted y'all to be here to hear dis so when they fuck up and I kill 'em… You won't be mad at me. You know what, you're right. So, you and her can go on and leave. BYE! But before y'all go, Ms. Baby Girl, don't think I didn't notice that sneaky-ass look in your eyes," Cha-Cha said as she stared at Baby Girl.

"Mama, there you go trippin'! What is you talking about woman? I ain't opened my mouth the whole time!" Baby Girl explained.

"Bitch, how many times I gotta tell you, I know you better than you know your damn self, so stop playin' me like I'm stupid or somethin'. I'm the one that had your red-ass, I keep telling you that. I know you waiting on me to fuck up so you can get your rocks off on me, but I'll never give you the satisfaction of getting your nut off on me! Now go on and get the fuck outta my face."

"What the fuck eva, Mama! I'm gone! Come on Sheila, let's get da hell on, 'cause this woman done lost her damn mind," Baby Girl said while rolling her eyes and her neck at the same time.

"Shawty, y'all too much alike, dat's why you can't get along for shit. I ain't takin no sides, but dat girl ain't said nothing da whole time we been in this kitchen, and right before she left, you snapped on her for no reason," Charlie said.

"I ain't snapped on her for no reason, I know what I saw. She can fool y'all, but she cai'n fool me. I ain't going for it-she got Droup wrapped around her little finger, but not me," Cha-Cha replied.

"Sidd, shawty, you wanna know da truth? She's just a red version of you, her mama. From what I've heard from the family, she ain't no different from how you was when you was coming up in the streets. Now dat's you seeing yo-self all ova again, and you can't accept it. You know it's the truth," Charlie said, trying to reason with her.

"I don't wanna hear dat shit—Damn her! Anyway, Tyrone, my weed man, he hit me up earlier today talking about he got some good shit for me. He was talking about somethin' called 'Tie Stick.' He said dis shit cost $10 a joint," Cha-Cha explained. Nathan and Charlie stared at her in disbelief.

"$10 a joint!" Nathan said, "this shit better make me puke up my damn insides if I'm paying $10.00 a joint."

"God damn shawty, that's a lot for one little bitty ass joint. This shit here must have been grown on the Moon," Charlie said.

But little did they know, what they was about to get in their hands was about to change the weed game for a long time to come.

"That's what I said when he told me about it, but as we all know, he don't never keep nothing but the best shit around. He told me one joint will get at least 10 to 15 people higher than them smoking 3 joints to the head by themselves. If it's as good as he says it is, then I'll be pulling in a lot more money than what I'm getting now. My clientele will grow and spread like springtime flowers. So that means I'll be able to finally put y'all in the positions that I've been waiting to. I will be able to fall back a little, but not much since I still gotta keep an eye on you two," Cha-Cha explained.

"When are we expecting this weed? 'Cause I can't wait to smoke me some of this shit, so I can see what he's talking about. Ain't that right, homeboy?" Nathan said.

"Shidd, you already know I'm ready to smoke me one," Charlie replied.

"Well he's out of town right now, but as soon as he gets in town, he's supposed to come by here and bring me some so I can let some of my people test it. Only thing he keep stressing to me is not to try and smoke the whole joint at one time, now; he said just take two or 3 puffs, and put it out. Ain't no way in hell this shit is that powerful," Cha-Cha said.

"Well I know one thing, you need to call or page his ass. Tell him he needs to hurry up and get here so I can try me some of that moon reefer," Nathan said as everyone started laughing.

"Damn straight shawty, and if it's as crunk as he says it is, then that's what we're going to call it, the Moon Reefer," Charlie and Nathan said at the same time.

While she was still filling them in on her plans for the new weed she started moving around in the kitchen trying to finish getting dinner prepared for her hardworking husband. She reached under the sink and got the same cast iron skillet that Punkin had used to cook in. She was using it for the fried chicken so she got out some rice, corn meal, and an onion.

She was cooking one of everyone's favorite meals: some fried chicken, rice and gravy, sweet corn bread, and a pitcher of red Kool-Aid. When she went to get the utensils, Nathan and Charlie went to the kitchen table and took a seat and listened and watched at the same time. One thing everyone knew about Cha-Cha, whether she was in the kitchen cooking or bagging up reefer, she meant business and took it very seriously. One of her favorite sayings was, "I don't play the radio, and if the TV gets too loud, I'll shoot that bitch." The funny thing about it, and they knew it, she meant every word of it.

"Say lil lady," Nathan said from the kitchen table, "I know you got us something to smoke, so go ahead and pull out one of your cigarette packs so we can smoke us one while we wait on dinner to get cooked."

"Don't think your ass is going to get high and eat up everything, plus who the hell is We? I don't speak French mother-fucker," she replied.

"I know you don't, but I sure the hell do, 'we oh la la' and all that shit they be saying," Nathan responded. Everyone in the kitchen just burst out laughing.

"Here boy, take this and light one up witcho crazy ass," Cha-Cha said, handing him a cigarette pack full of nut'n but rolled up joints that she usually keeps for herself to smoke on.

Chapter 6

s Punkin was outside in the front yard, the only thing he could think about was that dude he saw dead earlier that day. He kept remembering the way he looked laying there on the ground dead, with blood all over his body. With that thought in his head, the only thing he could hear was his big brother Nathan saying, "Another man looks a whole lot better laying there with flowers growing on him than you do. So, if you can help it, don't let no fucking body kill you, you hear me? Shit, it's better for you to be judged by 12 than carried by six any day." Even though Punkin's mama didn't want him to hurt anyone, because she said it makes him heartless, he would refuse to let anyone hurt him if he could help it. Plus, Punkin thought about what it was like living in Carver Homes Projects and how it felt to be jumped as many times as he had been. It had built up hate inside of him. Punkin was so deep in thought and longing for the day to come for him to kill one of the niggas that jumped him that he didn't even notice his big brother Nathan coming out of the apartment until he heard the screen door close. He looked up and saw Nathan standing on the front porch.

"Come on lil nigga, "Nathan said. Punkin immediately took off running back to the front porch to see what his big brother wanted. They both sat down.

"What's on your mind, shawty?" Nathan asked. "Don't try to lie to me, because you had a real serious look on your face. If I ain't know no better, I'd say you have murder on your lil bad-ass mind."

"How you know what I was thinking about?" Punkin asked.

"Nigga, I'm one of the ones who used to change your shitty ass pamper and wipe your snotty nose. So, I know that look when I see it. You had that same look on your face you always have before you attack, but who's these niggas you plannin' to kill?" Nathan asked.

"Some niggas on the next street and down the street. They always gotta jump me. I mean, I be fighting 'em back, but I can't beat up no two or three niggas at the same time. That's the reason why I can't wait to get old enough and buy me a gun so I can shoot'em all in the face." Punkin explained.

Nathan just stood there listening to Punkin talk with a smile on his face, because he knew Punkin was serious.

"It's gonna be a'ight." Nathan explained, "Trust me! Come sit down. It's time for us to have a real serious talk."

As they both sat down on the steps, Punkin noticed Nathan's face went from a smile to serious in a split second and Punkin had never noticed this look before. Or if he did, he didn't pay any attention 'til now. It was one of them looks that said, "This ain't the time to play or the time to joke, period," and if Punkin did, that was his ass.

"Wassup big bro," Punkin said as he sat down beside Nathan.

"So, you dun started sacking up weed now?" Nathan asked Punkin.

"Yeah, Mama let me sack up some wit her this morning, 'cause I told her she be putting too much in the bags. Why? Am I in trouble?" Punkin asked.

"Hell naw. Trouble for what? You ain't did nothing wrong. All of us ain't nothin' but some hustlers, so that just means it's naturally in your blood to be one. You already know my motto, "if it don't make dollars, it don't make sense," they both said at the same time.

"Mama just finished talking to me and Charlie about you. She's finally given me permission to go ahead and show you the ropes of how life really is out here in the streets. So, depending on what's going on tomorrow, I might be taking you with me. It ain't like you need a whole lot of learning anyway. Hell, most of it, you're picking up right here at home." Nathan explained.

"For real big brother? Because I'm sho is ready," Punkin told him.

"Yeah, for real, and I know you're ready; that's what I'm afraid of," Nathan admitted.

"That little nigga there is gonna be hell to tell the captain," Nathan thought to himself.

"So, I finally get the chance to go and hang out with my big brother! Shit, I can't wait till tomorrow comes. Hope he ain't got nothing to do," Punkin thought to himself.

"What we gonna do big brother?" Punkin asked Nathan.

"Don't worry about it, and don't start asking all them damn questions! And don't forget that's only if nothing else comes up," Nathan explained.

"All right!" Punkin responded.

"Now go on and play....... might be the last time you get the chance to play," Nathan said.

"Who? I only play the radio, and if the TV gets too loud, I shoot that bitch," Punkin responded. As he got up, he smelled fried chicken cooking.

Ok lil nigga, I really hope you know what that means, 'cause from now on, you'll live by them words. So, after today, the first time I catch you playing with anybody or smiling at anybody--- dat's your ass. You hear me, nigga, "Nathan asked.

"Yeah," Punkin responded.

"One more thing… The reason why Mama's given me and Charlie, well me, permission to groom you out here is because she wants you to run this family business one day when she's old and gray," Nathan explained as Punkin walked in the apartment

When Punkin heard that, he stopped dead in his tracks, turned around, and looked at his big brother.

"Are you serious big bro?" he asked.

"As a fucking heart attack. Why else do you think I'd be telling you all dis if it wasn't true?"

In his heart, Punkin knew what Nathan was telling him the truth, because one thing he did know--- Nathan didn't play, especially when it came to their mama! For some reason, Punkin really couldn't believe what he was hearing, so he just stood there listening to Nathan finish talking.

"You and Enos are mama's favorite two kids. Don't get me wrong, she loves all us kids, but when it comes to y'all two--- her world revolves around y'all," Nathan explained.

"You been the one doing everything for her, and always around her. That's why I can't wait to get grown, so I can do whatever I wanna do," Punkin said.

"Look, don't be in no rush to get grown. Y'all are the last two babies she has left, so you especially, you better not disappoint her. Now she has everything riding on you, and if you do disappoint her, I will kill you myself, much as I love you; I ain't playing witchu either. Now go on in the house, and this conversation stays right here," Nathan said.

Punkin nodded nervously, because he knew Nathan meant every word he said. Then he turned back around to head inside and saw Charlie standing there with a smile on his face. So, Punkin smiled back at him, then Punkin went on past, but before he got clear, Charlie slapped Punkin upside his head.

Charlie told him, "You know I just heard y'all's conversation, right? What Nathan said was real--- you better not disappoint her."

"I ain't," Punkin assured.

"We don't play about her," Charlie reminded Punkin.

Punkin just stood there, not saying a word, just taking it all in, because one thing he knew, that 3 years from now, he'd be 13 years old. At that time, he would be well groomed and just about ready for whatever came his way. Charlie never said much; he was always a quiet one, so when he spoke, Punkin listened.

Charlie always stayed dope-boy fresh seven days a week. You'd never catch him not looking fresh. Like today, he had on some white and green Stan Smith Adidas, an all-white Adidas sweat suit with three green lines coming down both sides of his pants and on each side of the jacket sleeves. He also had on a green and white Adidas T shirt, not to mention, a big ass gold chain around his neck. Like the kind that rappers like LL Cool J, Run DMC and da Fat Boys were wearing in the music videos on MTV. The only difference is, theirs didn't have anything on the necklace, but he had a big lion on his, which Punkin thought meant Charlie was king of the jungle. As Punkin looked at him and listened to him thinking about Nathan, who was still sitting out on the front porch, Punkin knew he wanted to be just like them. One was a straight killa who didn't play no games. And the other was also a killer, but he would rather finesse the situation. But if he couldn't finesse it, then oh well, off witcha head.

Punkin thought to himself, "*I know no other child at ten years old that's getting the game I'm getting. What more could I ask for, I'm getting the best of both worlds.*"

Chapter 7

When Punkin finally walked past Charlie to the kitchen he noticed his mama was at the stove. He could have sworn she heard their conversation, but then again, he doubted it seriously. When Nathan speaks, he never raises his voice, even when he's mad, plus she was so deep in thought, she didn't even hear him walk up behind her.

"Mama," Punkin said.

"What boy?" his mama responded.

"What's wrong witchu?" Punkin asked her.

"Nothing's wrong. I'm just deep in thought right now, 'cause I got a lot on my mind, dat's all. Go upstairs and check on your little brother; he's been up there asleep for a long time now," Cha-Cha told him.

"Yes ma'am," Punkin responded.

As Punkin was going upstairs to check on his little brother, he heard some loud music outside in front of their apartment. It was one of his favorite songs. He sat on the steps to be sure he was hearing right as it got louder. It was

Run DMC; it was their song called "King of Rock." He took off running to the top of the stairs and stood on his tip toe so he can look out the window. Just like he had figured, it was JJ, and a smile came across his face like it was Christmas time. JJ always let him go with him, and not to mention, he was another crazy-ass nigga who people feared like hell. Everyone called him "Crazy JJ". He would shoot you before God got the news, and he stayed with a big pistol wherever he went. Soon as Punkin saw who it was, he took off running to Sheila's room and banged on her door.

"Boyyy, you better stop banging on my door like you goddamn crazy," Sheila screamed as she snatched open her door, "you know this damn baby is in here asleep," she added.

He paid her no attention and ran straight past to where Baby Girl was sitting and told her JJ was outside. She then got up with a big smile on her face and left the room to go downstairs to meet him. As soon as she walked out, Enos woke up looking crazy like, "what's going on?"

"See what the fuck you done did… You just had to bring your ass up here and wake up this damn boy," Sheila said.

"Mama told me to come up here an' check on him anyway," Punkin responded.

"You and Mama startin' to get on my damn nerves! Plus, who the fuck you think you getting smart wit? I will beat your lil ass nigga, 'cause you damn sure ain't grown yet, and you gonna respect me! You hear me, boy?" Sheila replied.

"Yes, big sister. I'm sorry," Punkin replied.

"Don't be sorry, be careful. Now come here and give me a big hug," Sheila told him.

He went and gave his big sister a hug, because he knew she was the one who didn't play when she got mad, her or Samantha. Baby Girl, on the other hand, wasn't talking about shit, far as he was concerned. She was his big sister, and he respected her to a point, but she stayed into it with their mama a lot. So that alone made him lose all respect for her. After he hugged Sheila, he grabbed his little brother, and they went downstairs.

"JJ is here lil bro," Punkin said as they were going downstairs.

Fo' weal, big bwudda?" Enos excitedly projected, surprised with a big smile on his face.

"Yep," Punkin said as they went downstairs into the living-room where everyone was kickin' it, except for Mama. She was still in the kitchen trying to finish up dinner before their daddy got home from work.

As they entered the living room JJ said, "There goes my two lil niggas right there. Wassup y'all?"

"Wuddup JJ?" Enos returned, smiling.

"You been bein' bad and kicking ass like you supposed to lil nigga? 'Cause if you ain't, I'm finna beat your ass," JJ joked with Enos.

"Man, pweeze ou don't wan' nonna me," Enos responded, giving him "five" as he said it.

Hearing him, JJ and everyone else just started laughing.

"See, that's why he's so damn bad now. Y'all gonna make sure y'all corrupt both of'em, ain't cha?" Baby Girl said.

"Girl, shut the hell up! What you want them to be, pussies? As long as I'm around, it ain't gonna happen," JJ said, looking at Baby Girl.

Punkin just stood there for a few minutes listening and watching the scene before he asked, "Wassup my nigga? Can I go outside and listen to your radio?"

"Hell, naw! That's all your ass think about whenever he comes over," Baby Girl said, before JJ could reply.

"Bitch, you better leave my mother-fucking baby alone, 'cause he wasn't talking to yo stankin ass anyway. And you don't own no fucking car to be tellin' nobody shit about shit!" Cha-Cha yelled from the kitchen.

"Damn, ma! I was just playing with his lil ass. That's why he don't have no respect for me now, because every time I say some'n to'm, you gotta say some'n," Baby Girl responded.

"Well, don't say shit to him then," Cha-Cha responded.

"He's still my damn lil brother too, and don't forget before you stopped getting drunk, who used to take care of him," Baby Girl fired back.

"So, fucking what? I don't get drunk no mo', so you ain't gonna do shit else for him again. Hell, he might have to take care of yo' ass one day," Cha-Cha shot back with anger in her eyes.

Nathan, Charlie, and JJ just sat there listening and smiling, because this was an everyday thing between mother and daughter. Just today alone, they had already bumped heads umpteen times.

"I sho will be glad when my daddy gets here so he can calm your ass down," Baby Girl said.

"What the fuck he gonna do? He ain't my damn daddy! You better hope I don't put both of y'all damn asses out together," Cha-Cha yelled back at her.

As soon as Cha-Cha finished making her statement, their daddy pulled up on the side of the apartment. Baby Girl looked out the window to make sure it was him and started smiling.

"There goes my daddy!" she said. Baby Girl knew that if no one else was on her side, he'd have her back. No matter what anyone said, she could do no wrong by him. She jumped right up and ran out the front door to meet him. She gave him a big hug. He looked like he was tired from working long hours in a hot and sweaty shop where he worked on tires all day long. He was dressed in his usual, all blue uniform. He wore it five, sometimes seven, days a week. It had his name, Jonas Love, stitched over his right top pocket, and the company name, "Peterson Tires", stitched over the left. He had been working for them for 15 years, so he could take care of his family. The whole family seemed to know that Baby Girl always acted like a big two-year-old baby whenever she was around her daddy.

Cha-Cha just stood in the kitchen window looking out at Baby Girl and her husband with an evil eye. She could just imagine what all she was out there saying to him before he could even get inside the front yard, not to mention the apartment. *"That little bitch think she got all the fuckin' sense. I got something for both they asses,"* Cha-Cha thought to herself as she continued to watch on. They must have felt her watching, because they both looked up at the same time and saw her lookin with a very evil look on her face.

She knew Droup was going to say something to her as soon as he walked in the door. But what the hell did she care. This was her castle, and she was the head queen in charge, and whoever didn't like it could kiss her ass! Or they could get the hell on, as far as she was concerned. It was always her way or the highway--- either way, it didn't matter to her.

The front screen door opened, and Droup and Baby Girl walked into the kitchen. At first, they just stood there looking at each other.

"Wat da fuck you standin there lookin at me stupid for?" Cha-Cha asked.

"You know good goddamn well why I'm looking at you. Why in the hell you keep messin wit dis damn girl? Ain't I done told you to leave her alone? I'm gettin' tired of coming home to hearing about this shit every day. And what's this shit I hear about you letting this boy bag up some goddamn reefer?" Droup asked.

"First of all, I'm sick and fucking tired of that lil red bitch always running to you like you <u>my</u> goddamn daddy or somethin'! This my goddamn apartment, and if she don't like it, she can go on upstairs and pack her shit, 'cause I don't give a fuck. The same thing goes for you too, 'cause you can't whip my ass and neither can she," Cha-Cha snapped at Droup.

"You done lost your goddamn mind. I ain't goin' no damn where and neither is she. And answer my damn question… What's dis I hear about you lettin' dis boy bag up reefer? Punkin! Bring yo' ass here, boy!" Droup yelled.

"Sir?" Punkin responded as he started walking to the kitchen doorway. His daddy just stood there looking down at him like he was about to kill him.

Punkin was so scared, you could see the sweat had started forming on his forehead. Like everyone else in the family, Punkin was scared of his daddy. Before the time Punkin was even born, his daddy had been locked up twice for murder and no telling for what else. As for Droup, he didn't talk much, so when he did say something, everyone else fell silent like the cat had their tongue. Punkin walked up to his daddy with his head down, taking baby steps, because he didn't know what to expect.

Then he heard Baby Girl say, "Didn't I tell you I was going to tell daddy on your lil bad ass, huh?"

Punkin raised his head with so much anger in his eyes that if Satan, himself, was standing there, he'd be proud of Punkin . *"I'ma kill your ass one day for snitching on me bitch,"* he was thinking the whole time, looking at his sister.

"What the fuck you doing putting your goddamn hands on some reefer?" Droup asked Punkin. But before Punkin could open his mouth, Cha-Cha snapped on both of them.

"Leave him a-motherfucking-lone, and you ain't gon' put your goddamn hands on him. I told him to do it--- so if you got anything to say, say it to me! That's why I can't stand that lil red bitch, 'cause all she know how to do is run to you and start shit. Like you gon' whoop somebody's ass or some'n! Who the fuck he's suppose to be? Huh? Why you run telling him every motherfucking thing? Y'all scared of his motherfucking ass! Not me! Matter of fact, both of y'all get the fuck outta my motherfucking kitchen with this bullshit so I can finish cooking my dinner. You can go on back there baby and finish doing whatever you was doin'." Cha-Cha said to Punkin.

"Yes ma'am," Punkin said while looking at Baby Girl, smiling and shooting her the bird as he turned and went back into the living-room.

"Wassup Daddy?" everyone said at the same time as Droup walked through the living room, headed upstairs to his bedroom. Everyone knew he wasn't going to say nothing back to any of them. Not that he was mad, it was just that he barely said anything to anybody. But he did acknowledge them with a head nod. As soon as he was out of sight and Baby Girl sat down, Nathan got on her ass.

"Girl, you gotta be the stupidest child Mama got. I don't understand you for shit in the world. Why in the hell would you run outside to Daddy telling him on Mama and Punkin? You know who run this damn house! You of all people know how Mama feel about those too damn boys. You just ain't gonna be satisfied till she fuck you up, and who you think going to get in her way or stop her? No damn body, that's who!" Nathan said, looking at Baby Girl as he spoke.

Baby Girl just sat there, not saying a word. She knew what her big brother was telling her was the truth. Nobody got in Cha-Cha's way when she got mad. She was like a lil fuckin tornado, fucking up everything in her way like the Tasmanian devil., only this wasn't a cartoon.

"Don't tell her shit else, Nathan. Matter of fact, JJ you better get her stankin ass out of my house before I come in there and slap her ass with one of my butcher knives," Cha-Cha threatened.

"Come on, girl! Get yo' shit and let's go with your crazy ass! I can't even come over here and chill for a few hours, 'cause you wanna go and start some shit wit yo' mama! You know everybody in y'all fucking family, except y'all daddy, is a street nigga and a hustler. That's all Punkin's coming up around. So what the fuck you expect from him? From the day he was born, it was in him. Some was blessed with it, but he was born with it. A'ight y'all, I'll catch you later, let me take her ass outta here, 'cause she just won't learn. Gimme a minute", JJ said as he walked toward the kitchen.

"I know you finishing up dinner, and I hate to miss out, but we gonna go and pick up somethin' to eat from the plaza. It's already smellin good too, so y'all enjoy with your husband. We'll be a'ight." JJ said as he prepared to leave with Baby Girl.

He attempted to hug Cha-Cha goodbye, but she did an about face and told him, "You ain't gotta go out and get her nothin to eat, just get her ass outta here away from me for about an hour so I can calm the fuck down and finish cookin'. 'Cause if you don't! Anyway, we all go'n eat dinner wit Droup. He been out all day work in' and I don't want him trippin' when he come downstairs and she gone without sayin' nothin', even though I don't really give a fuck." He just laughed and gave her a big hug anyway and went back to the living room.

"You ready Crazy Girl? That's yo' new name!..fuck Baby Girl. Let's go out and get some fresh air for a minute so all y'all can just simmer down while yo mama still simmering that good ass food for dinner. We'll come back when it's safe. See y'all, we out for a little bit." JJ told them as he dapped all of'em then scooped up Baby Girl and headed towards the door.

"Daddy....." Baby Girl called upstairs.

"Daddy!" She yelled up the stairs the second time.

"Yeah, Baby Girl?" Droup answered.

"I'm going' out for a minute...I'll be back before dinner." Said Baby Girl.

"OK, baby," Droup acknowledged.

On the way to the car, JJ apologized for being so hard on her.

Cha-Cha finished dinner in about an hour and set the table for Droup and called him downstairs when she heard the front door opening. It was Baby Girl and JJ right on time for dinner. It was awkward, because hardly anybody said anything. A couple of icebreakers were attempted by the boys, but there was still tension between the ladies and Droup. So they all ate pretty much in silence then praised and thanked Cha-Cha for dinner. That may have been best, all things considered. Tomorrow would be a brand new day with brand new attitudes.

Chapter 8

Ring! Ring! Ring!

"Hello?" Cha-Cha answered.

"Is Cha-Cha there?" the caller inquired.

"This me," she replied.

"Wassup baby, this Tyrone. I'm back in town, and I'm getting ready to come your way with the new-new I got for you."

"Well, I can't wait for you to come on over here, 'cause I'm ready to pitch a bitch at 11:30, so make sure you bring your camera, 'cause I damn sho' got mines," Cha-Cha told him.

"Ok baby, see you soon," Tyrone told her.

As they ended the call, she immediately went to adding up the money she was about to get now, if everything went right. She was looking at getting thousands on top of thousands in cold hard cash, especially with the clientele she already had. She was moving anywhere from 1 to 2 pounds a day, and that was just with nickel and dime bags, not considering what she makes when her country boys from outta town places an order--- hell, that right there was at least 3 to 8 more pounds. Now it was just a matter of marketing it, which she knew from experience would be a piece of cake, or in other words, like taking candy from a baby. She was sitting, smiling to herself, so deep in thought that she didn't hear when Tyrone pulled up in his dune buggy out front. He had plenty of money, but you could never tell, because he always kept a low profile to keep the police off of him. If you didn't know him personally, you'd never know he was the man with so many pounds.

He got out of his car with his Louis Vuitton pouch in his hand. He completely caught Cha-Cha off guard when he knocked, because she was so deep in thought.

Knock! Knock! Knock!

"Who is it?" Cha-Cha asked, glancing down at her watch to see that 45 minutes had passed by so quickly.

"Tyrone"

"Heeyyyyy babbbbyyyy wasssuuuppp?!!" she said as she opened the front door to let him in as they greeted each other with a hug.

"So, let me see what you got for me, 'cause the way you was talkin' 'bout this shit, you got everybody in the house anxious," Cha-Cha told him.

He just went right on into the living room, smiling to himself, as if he knew what he just had come through the door with was the best shit in all of Georgia. Fuck Atlanta, because that was just a very small portion of the state of Georgia. He already knew that with this lady sitting in the living room with him on his team, he would have a very nice part of the city of Atlanta in no time. And just think of the other spots she was already serving, like Virginia, South and North Carolina and a few spots in the backwoods. She helped him move more than 10 to 15 pounds a week or two of his own when she was out of stock or just to help him out.

"Who's here to help you with this shit, 'cause you're going to need some help," he said dropping a piece of aluminum foil on the table in the living room, rolled up like a joint. She picked it up, looking at it.

"What the hell is this?" She said holding the foil between two fingers with a quizzical look on her face.

"Open it up and see," Tyrone told her.

When she opened it up, she noticed a joint inside looking like it was dipped in some type of oil or something, or maybe it was wet from water. It was so oily, she really couldn't believe what she was seeing.

"What da hell is dis?" Cha-Cha asked.

"Tie Stick," he told her.

"Tie Stick?" she asked, not believing him at first.

"Yep."

"Man, wait 'til my sons see this shit right here," she told Tyrone.

"As a matter of fact, where they at anyway?" Tyrone asked.

"Upstairs sleep. Oh, don't worry about it. They 'bout to get they asses up right now. Nathan! Charlie! Get y'all asses down here! Tyrone is down here with this new shit," she called out.

A few minutes later they both came downstairs, smiling, ready to see what all the talk was about.

"Wassup my nigga," Charlie said, walking ova to Tyrone to shake his hand. Nathan on the other hand just sat down and nodded his head saying,

"Sup?"

Soon as they both sat down, Cha-Cha gave the foil to Nathan. When he opened it up and saw it, the first thing that came out of his mouth was, "Damn nigga, what you do, drop this shit in some water or something?"

Tyrone just started laughing, "Yep..or somethin," then he passed it to Charlie.

"This shit looks like it's wet or something," Nathan added. Charlie reached and grabbed the foil from Nathan. As soon as he did, the first thing that came to his mind was a bunch of melted down crack.

"What the hell did you do to this shit nigga, melt a bunch of crack down and dip this shit in it?" Charlie asked. As soon as he said that, they all burst out laughing.

"Hell naw my nigga, this shit here is Tie Stick, and I'm willing to bet it is way better than them geek joints you be smoking. As a matter of fact, here, take my lighter and light it up. But don't be greedy and think that shit is something to play with, because you 'Will' pay for it! I promise you dat," Tyrone said, handing Charlie his lighter.

Charlie grabbed the lighter from him to fire up the joint, and as soon as he fired it up and inhaled the smoke, he started choking uncontrollably. He kept choking for almost a full minute before he was able to utter a single word. Everybody in the room started laughing as he choked his head off.

"This shit smokin' like hell," he said passing the joint and lighter to Nathan when he grabbed them from him and put the fire back on it. He got the same result after just one hit.

"Shiiit shawty, I'm high as a motherfucker, and I didn't hit it but once. This shit here is about to take over the world as far as the weed game goes," Charlie said.

Nathan was finally able to speak after coughing like hell and still coughing as he tried to speak.

"I don't know what dis shit is, but one thing for sho, I'm not fucking calling this shit Tie Stick. I'm calling this shit Moon Reefer, because this shit gets you higher than the fuckin' moon," he said with smoke still in his lungs and coughing. Instantaneously, the room filled with laughter.

"Let me see that damn joint and lighter so I can see for myself. I knowed y'all ass still got virgin lungs," Cha-Cha said while grabbing the joint and lighter from Nathan. As soon as she put the fire on the joint again and inhaled, she got the same results, but it took her a full minute and some change before she could speak again. She caught it the worst out of everybody, because she was the oldest and been smoking before the kids were born. Tyrone just sat there the whole time with a big ass smile on his face, enjoying the scene.

"Hell, yeah! Now I see what they talking about. I'm loving this shit right here. I'm so ready to start moving this shit. I gotta start calling my clientele and let'em know I got some of the best shit ever...that one hitter quitter," Cha-Cha ranted and raved optimistically still trying to catch her breath.

"Hahahahahahahahahaha! I told y'all dat dis shit ain't no joke. Ya'll still got half a joint left, and ain't nobody tried to grab it to light it back up. Dat one right there will last y'all til at least 5 o'clock. Now since you see what it is and you love it, like I knew you would…I'll be right back," Tyrone said, as he walked briskly to his car.

When he returned, he had a big brown grocery sack in his hands. He sat on the living room floor with the bag between his legs. He opened it up, reached in and pulled out some of the greenest and oiliest reefer any of them had laid eyes on. The smell that came from it was five times stronger than anything they had ever smelled coming from some reefer. He usually charged her $600 for a pound of weed, but this wasn't just any type of weed. This was the ultimate, the Big Brother of all weed.

He handed her a pound so she could look at it. As soon as she did, her 'Get Money' wheel started churning out ridiculous numbers, lighting up her face like fireworks. She was feeling good as can be off just one hit and seemingly a million coughs. It was time to put her master plan into full effect.

"What's it going to cost me? I already know it's probably going to be around $1200 just from guessing," Cha-Cha said.

"Damn, you're good. You hit it right on the head," Tyrone told her.

"OK, so how many of these pretty ass bags you brought with you in that grocery bag?" she asked him.

"I didn't bring nothing but four with me," he responded.

"I want all of 'em. Hold on, I'll be right back."

She went upstairs to her bedroom, looked under her mattress, and grabbed the brown Gucci pouch filled with money. She only needed one, because it contained $6000 to the penny. She left the other three pouches under the mattress and headed back downstairs. On her way back down, she was thinking to herself about the power move to come in the next few weeks and months. But for now, she was satisfied.

"Here, this is $6000," she said as she handed him the pouch, "you owe me one more pound, but I ain't in no hurry for it, not unless this shit moves faster than I expect it to," she said.

"OK, but you'll have it soon, 'cause I know you'll be calling me in a few days. One thing I love about you so much is when you see an opportunity, you take it with full force."

"I know I do," Cha-Cha thought to herself, but she didn't dare say it out loud.

"You gonna count your money, honey?" Cha-Cha asked.

"For what? One thing I know about you--- if you say it's $6000, then that's what it is. Not a penny less, it might be a few pennies over, but never less, so I don't see a need to count," Tyrone gracefully stated in trust.

He opened up the brown Gucci pouch, grabbed the knots of money in the rubber bands, put it in his own Louis Vuitton pouch, and handed hers back.

"Oh yeah and one more thing before I go. Make sure you keep that refer cool. I don't know why, but that's just how it works," Tyrone instructed.

"OK. Glad you let me know, Cha-Cha said, then turned to Nathan and Charlie and asked, "why in the fuck is both of y'all sitting over there looking stupid? Get y'all's asses up and help me get this shit together."

"Mama, what time you gonna cook breakfast? I'm hungry as hell," Nathan said.

"I'ma break your ass real fast, if you don't do what the fuck I told you to do. Now get your ass up right now," Cha-Cha said.

"I'll see you later Cha-Cha. I gotta go make more stops," Tyrone said, then he added to Nathan and Charlie, "Y'all like that, I take it?"

All Nathan and Charlie could do was sit there and look stupid.

"OK, call me later or I might be hitting you up on your hip after I make a few calls. You know I'ma be charging anywhere from $1500 to $1700 a pound, just so you know. Now, let me get in there and cook them some breakfast and make some calls," Cha-Cha told him.

"See you later," Tyrone said, heading for the door.

"Bye, sugga," Cha-Cha called after him.

When Tyrone left, Cha-Cha locked the screen door and the front door behind him. Then she turned and went to make sure that the back door and its screen door were locked too. After checking all the doors, she went into the kitchen where Nathan and Charlie were. They had gotten the scissors, bags, aluminum foil, and her scale, and were sitting at the kitchen table ready to be put to work. Everyone was high beyond belief, but everyone was focused. She told them what to do while she started to cook breakfast, making her calls at the same time. No matter how much business she had to handle, she always made sure she fed her kids, even though they were grown.

She had stopped getting drunk 2 years prior, because she got tired of it, and now she was about to build one of the strongest empires any woman had ever built from absolutely nothing. And she was well on her way.

She gave perfect instructions on how she wanted everything done, while she was on the phone putting out the word on her new batch. She was telling them the prices and at first everyone was like, "What the hell type reefer did she have to be charging $10 a joint, $75 to $100 for half an ounce, and $150-$200 for a whole ounce?" She put her word on it, and told everybody it was worth it. She made sure they understood it was a "one hitter quitter."

Before she knew it, everybody she had called was placing orders for at least 3 ounces or more. It was 11:45 AM, and by the time 5 o'clock rolled around, she only had 16 ounces left out of 64. It was moving so fast that it shocked even her. She had made $9,600 in no time, and she was making $3,200 a pound with each ounce going at $200 apiece. Just like she knew, she had no complaints at all. She called Tyrone at 6pm that night and told him she needed 5 more pounds, because all she had left was a pound. She knew that would be gone by that night or in the morning, seeing as her people kept hitting her back placing more orders. Everyone was loving this new reefer. He just sat on the other end of the line listening and thinking to himself, "*I might as well front her five more pounds after she buys her five, because she is gonna get it gone ASAP.*"

"Ok. I'll be through there in the morning with your 6 pounds. What do you think about me fronting you 5 more of these?" he asked.

"Shit, come on wit it; you know I'm 'bout that money!" Cha-Cha responded, excited about the prospect of making even more profit.

Ok, then. Be there in the morning with eleven of 'em for you. One more thang girl, how you do it?"

"It just come natural is all I can say," Cha-Cha told him.

"That it does. See you in the morning."

With that, they both hung up.

Chapter 9

One month after Cha-Cha had been selling Tie Stick, everything was starting to look up for her. The money was better now, just like she knew it would be. Nobody had her connections, and if there was someone else, they were in another state. So, Tyrone was her own little secret. She had a niche market. Everyone was loving Tie Stick, couldn't get enough of it. No one had any idea that he was just taking the weed that he had and spraying it with a special fluid to increase the high of the reefer. And now it was time for him to play the drought game and let his lady get her money up to the max. But little did he know, Cha-Cha knew the game herself, and was preparing for it on the low, even though she didn't see it coming. She already had started stashing away a pound or two every time she re-upped with him. So, she had 8 pounds hidden at her Samantha's apartment. Nobody else but the two of them knew about it. One thing about Cha-Cha, she always thought two steps ahead. She knew if a drought was coming, she could get double what she was getting before.

Depending on how much she had at the time would determine how she would sell it. It wouldn't be in pounds, only $50 sacks consisting of only 5 or maybe 6 joints.

For some reason, she was in a very good mood on Friday. She was smiling from ear to ear and had even been joking with people. She felt like doing something special that night, like having a little get together. She figured that would be fun, so she picked up the phone and started dialing.

"Hello?" Samantha answered.

"What you doing?" Cha-Cha asked.

"Nut'n, 'bout to fix me some lunch."

"Ok, well I want you to come through here tonight, because I'm having a lil get together," Cha-Cha invited.

"What's the special occasion lil lady?" Samantha asked.

"Me, lil girl."

"Ok then, Ms. Me. I'll be over there."

"You better! You already been gone to Job Corp for months, and we ain't really spent any time together," Cha-Cha pointed out.

"I know. I'll be over there, Mama. Do I need to brang anything when I come?" Samantha asked.

"Naw, just you!"

"Ok, Mama. See you later then. Bye."

"Bye, baby."

When Cha-Cha hung up the phone, she made more calls to invite some of the people over that she was closest to. She had bought cases of Miller High Life Beer and placed an order for her special pills she called "T's", which were small, yellow pills. They were going to play Spades, Pollyanna, and maybe some Dominos. She pulled out some rib eye steaks, ribs, chicken wings, hamburger meat, and some hot dogs. She had planned on grilling everything except for the fish--- that she would deep fry. She was getting her plan together when she noticed a small white Toyota pull up on the side of her apartment with two white boys in the front seat and someone else in the back. When the passenger side door opened and the backseat was up, she noticed her oldest child, Smooth, was getting out of it. She immediately thought "*What the fuck do he want?*" At that time, there wasn't anybody at home except her and Nathan, who was upstairs watching TV. She knew Smooth was always bad news whenever he came around, and she didn't trust 'em out of her eye sight. She knew him well enough to know he would steal the stank offa shit if you blinked or turned your back on him.

"Nathan!!!" Smooth heard her yell from outside the apartment as he was approaching.

"Ma'am??" Nathan responded.

"That no good Smooth just showed up."

"Ok," Nathan replied. He knew, just like everyone else knew, how she felt about Smooth, and he stayed out of it until told to do otherwise. Everyone knew not to fuck with Cha-Cha, 'cause she would shoot you or cut the shit out of you. She was like a lil small piece of dynamite.

KNOCK! KNOCK! KNOCK! KNOCK!

"Boy, what the fuck do you want?" Cha-Cha asked, opening the door.

"Damn, Mama. You act like you ain't happy to see your son," Smooth replied.

"Nigga, I ain't ever happy to see yo' ass, because every time you come around, it's some bullshit wit you. And who the fuck is them two goddamn white boys you got out there on the side of my apartment?"

"They strait, Mama. They my buddies."

"Hell, for all I know they could be the goddamn police, and yo stankin' ass came by tryin' to set me up or somethin'.'"

"Mama, they ain't the damn police. Is you goin' to let me in so I can take a shit and be back on my damn way?" Smooth asked.

"Why you didn't take a shit in the woods somewhere? Hold on, I'm thinking. Just stay right there. I'll be back," Cha-Cha responded while blocking his way inside.

"Mama, just let me shit and I'm gone," he pleaded.

Something told her to say "Hell Naw", but she went against her better judgement in the situation, 'cause there wasn't anything for him to steal anyway. Plus, Nathan was upstairs in her bedroom.

"Come on in, go take you a shit, and then get the fuck outta my goddamn house, because you know I don't trust you at all," Cha-Cha told him.

When he came in, he tried to hug her, but she pushed him away.

"Damn, I can't hug my own mama?"

"Hell, naw you ain't gonna hug me smelling like a damn ho-bo, and look at you... You really look so damn bad, that shit is fucking you up good."

"Hell, you don't love me," Smooth told her.

"You don't love your goddamn self," she replied.

"Ok. Who's here with you?" Smooth asked.

"Don't be questioning me about who's in my goddamn house boy. Anyway, I thought you had to shit. Either go shit or back the fuck up, and get the fuck out my house right damn now," Cha-Cha warned him.

Without another word, Smooth went on upstairs and ran into Nathan coming out of the bathroom. Nathan hated to see him this way, because at one point in his life, Smooth had it going on. He had a good job, a good woman by his side, and a couple of cars. But now, nobody could understand what had happened to him because he was the total opposite.

"Wass up Smooth,"

"Shit, wassup Nathan"

"Boy, you mean to tell me that mama let you up these stairs? I find that hard to believe," Nathan said to Smooth.

"You know I caught all kinds of hell before I even got in the apartment. I see ain't nut'n changed. But let me go on so I can go. You the only one up here?" Smooth asked Nathan.

"Hell yeah. I'm in Mama's room watchin TV."

"Aight, let me go on and shit before she starts raising hell again."

"Aight, bet. You need to start back takin' better care of yourself." Nathan told him.

With that, Smooth headed into the bathroom and Nathan headed into the bedroom to finish watching "Good Times." Two minutes later Smooth came out of the bathroom and went into the bedroom where Nathan was. Nathan noticed him sweating real bad and acting like he was about to faint, leaning up against the door. But it was all part of the plot. Smooth purposefully splashed water on his face to make Nathan think something was wrong, and he knew to act like he was about to faint to get him out of the room.

"Damn, boy. You alright?" Nathan asked Smooth.

"Hell naw. For some reason I just got real hot and started sweating bad as hell, feeling like I'm about to faint," Smooth responded, holding on to the wall for support.

"Sit down before you fall out!"

"Aight, but I need a glass of ice water. Will you please go downstairs and get me a glass?"

"I gotcha. I'll be right back," Nathan told him.

As soon as Nathan left the room, Smooth went and lifted up the mattress and grabbed the brown Gucci pouch that was under there and tucked it in his pants under his shit. When Nathan was heading back upstairs with the glass of ice water and got to the top of the steps, Smooth was standing at the top. He told Nathan he was feeling better now and had to go before his ride left him.

Cha-Cha was in the kitchen when he was on his way out.

"Nathan just told me you wasn't feeling good. Said you was up there sweating real bad and about to faint." The whole time she spoke, she was eyeing him suspiciously, because she had a feeling something wasn't right.

"Yeah, I was, but it's passed over now. I don't know what was wrong with me, but I gotta go. Thank you, Mama," Smooth said as he walked out the door.

As soon as he walked out the door, Cha-Cha thought about her money that she had upstairs under her mattress and she knew he had stolen it. She could feel it.

"Nathan, check under my mattress and make sure my money is still there," Cha-Cha called out.

A few seconds later she heard Nathan coming down the steps like a bat outta hell, and she knew for sure her money was gone

"Mama, that motherfucker done stole it. Fuck! I should've known better than to trust that pussy ass nigga. I'ma kill 'em," Nathan said, seething with anger.

"Before he could finish getting it out, Cha-Cha had gone back in the kitchen and was on the phone calling the most dangerous killas she had on her team: JJ, DeWayne, and Harold, but they called him Dirty Harold, because he put you in the mind of Clint Eastwood with his .44 Magnum. Nathan was standing still when she got off the phone, mad as hell.

"How much did this bitch ass steal, Mama?" Nathan asked.

"It wasn't nut'n but $1,575, but it's the fucking principle of the shit. I let his goddamn ass in against my better judgement, and he disrespected me. He fuckin stole from me," Cha-Cha raged, pacing back and forth like a caged tiger.

"I wish you would've followed your first mind! Damn!" Nathan yelled, hitting the wall in anger.

"We'll find him today. Don't worry about it," Cha-Cha reassured him.

"Easy for you to say. I'm the one who got tricked."

"What the hell you talkin' 'bout boy? We both got tricked, and plus he stole my damn money!"

"Yeah, you right, Mama!"

Everyone must have been in the neighborhood, or close by, because in thirty minutes they were all there ready to go find Smooth and do whatever Mama Cha-Cha wanted done. Harold had his .44 magnum in his hands when he walked in. JJ had his .357 magnum in his shoulder holster under his jacket, and Dewayne had his Uzi with a silencer in his tote bag. You could see in all of their faces that they were mad as hell as they stood there waiting on the word "go". Harold was the first to speak.

"Mama, please tell me how in the fuck you let him, of all people, come in here and steal from you."

"I know baby. That motha-fucka tricked me, said he had to shit, and I went for it," Cha-Cha responded.

"And nigga, where the hell was you at Nathan?" Harold asked.

"Hell, I was upstairs. The bastard came out of the bathroom sweating like a pig and acting like he was about to faint. Asked me to come down and get him a glass of water, and the rest is history. We both got fucked!" Nathan explained to the group.

"That's the fuckin' oldest trick in the book---the water on the face and faint game. Nathan, you should have known better than that shit, nigga. But don't worry about it. We'll find 'em and make 'em pay for it one way or a motherfucking other," Dewayne said.

"I can't believe this nigga. He done fucked up this time for real. I gotta shoot that bitch," JJ added in.

"I want y'all to go and find that son of a bitch and brang his ass to me. Matter of fact, naw don't bring him to me. Call me, so I can come to him. That nigga go'n pay for this shit. I don't know what the fuck done got into him, but I'm 'bout to get it out of 'em. Take Nathan with y'all and JJ stayin' here with me," she ordered.

As soon as she had finished talking they all headed out the door and got into Dewayne's car and took off to find Smooth. Cha-Cha then went and called her daughter Samantha.

"You know your motherfucking brotha Smooth just came over here and stole my damn money," Cha-Cha told her.

"Naw, Mama. He ain't did nut'n like that I know! How did that happen?" Samantha asked.

"It don't matter how it happened. Y'all just get ready to bury that bastard when I find'm. You can call Sheila and Baby Girl and let them know too." Cha-Cha added.

"Please don't hurt my brother Mama. You know that he is sick and needs help," Samantha begged.

"Fuck your brotha! And I'm about to help him alright with a bullet to his fucking head."

"Mama!"

"Don't 'Mama' me, girl. I should've killed that bastard when he was born."

"But that's your son," Samantha reprimanded.

"Dat ain't no fucking son of mine. Bye!" and she slammed down the receiver, leaving Samantha to wonder if she could stop her mama in time.

Chapter 10

Sheila was just walking through the front door when she caught the end of her mama's conversation on the phone. It sounded like she was extremely pissed off. She wondered what the hell was going on as she walked into the kitchen and noticed JJ at the table with his .357 in his hand.

"What's going on now, Mama? And don't tell me nothing, 'cause I just seen Harold's car and JJ's car outside. Plus, you got JJ sitting over there at the table, with his pistol in his hand, and looking like he is mad at the world," Sheila said, looking at her mama to try and figure out what was going on.

"Oh, I'll tell you what's wrong. That motherfucka, Smooth, just came over here and stole my goddamn money. That's what's wrong! I'm about to find him and kill his ass. Don't give me that shit about 'that's your son, 'cause if the bastard was my son, his stankin ass wouldn't have stolen from me," Cha-Cha justified with hatred in her voice.

"Dat damn boy done lost his mind. And I guess Harold, Dewayne, and Nathan are out hunting for him," Sheila said, shaking her head in disbelief, "have you told Samantha yet?"

"Yeah, but I'ma help them find him. I was just cursing out Samantha's ass as you walked in the door," Cha-Cha informed.

"Samantha's?"

"Hell yeah, Samantha. Don't act like you so damned surprised, hell, I curse her ass out, too....tryna defend that bastard."

"Yeah, you mad alright for you to curse out your baby, Samantha. So I'ma go on upstairs, 'cause he's your son, and if you wanna kill him, then I guess he'll just be one dead ass brotha of mines. Hell, he should've known better than to steal from you anyway."

Sheila looked at JJ, before she went upstairs, who was over there smiling with a smile that she knew all too well.

"Damn, nigga, you was just sitting over there mad when I first came in, now you got that motherfuckin' evil-ass smile on your face. You sick in the damn head, boy," Sheila told JJ as she turned to leave the room.

JJ just looked, continuing to smile at Sheila, not saying a word, so she turned and headed upstairs to her bedroom.

Meanwhile, Nathan, Harold, and DeWayne were now riding around looking for Smooth. They were all mad as hell, especially Nathan, 'cause he felt like he had to get Smooth since he was the one who got tricked.

"Man, do anybody know where the fuck this nigga be at?" Harold asked.

"Who the hell knows! He's a junkie---Them motherfuckaz be everywhere. But I know one thing, we ain't goin' back til we find 'em," DeWayne replied.

"One thing I do know though... He may be a junkie, but he's not stupid enough to be on this side of town where Cha-Cha know everybody," logically, Nathan interjected.

"You might be right, but we're going to check this side of town first anyway since we already on this side of town," DeWayne told him.

First, they hit Pryor Rd Plaza, putting the word out then they rode down through the Joyland apartments and houses, asking everyone had they seen Smooth. They told everyone that if they saw him to call them immediately, because this was an emergency situation. They also warned people not to say anything to Smooth about them looking for him. Then they rode through Lakewood Village, High Point, and South Atlanta houses. Once they couldn't find him on that side of town they decided to head over by Pittsburg and

Mechanicsville. They rode around until they ran into Charlie, since he lived on that side of town. Luck must have been on their side, because as soon as they hit Machanicsville, Nathan spotted Charlie.

"There go Charlie right there, DeWayne. Hit the horn, and pull over," Nathan said.

DeWayne hit the horn and pulled over.

Bebebebebebe   beeeeeep   beeeeep   bebebebebe beeeeep

Charlie turned around instantly, because there was only one person he knew who hit the horn like that, and that was DeWayne. He called it the pimp horn.

"Wasss up homeboy?" Harold said, getting outta the passenger side, lifting the seat up to let Nathan out, and DeWayne followed by getting out on the driver side.

"Out here trying to get it up shawty. Y'all already know. What the hell y'all doing out together? There's gotta be a problem. Is y'all about to kill a mutherfucka?" Charlie asked out of suspicion.

"Smooth pussy ass. Dat nigga came over to the apartment and stole Cha-Cha's money," Nathan told him.

"What the fuck! That nigga done lost his goddamn mind ain't he? Now I see why he was acting all strange and shit when I seen him," Charlie told the group.

"Where the fuck that nigga at?" Harold asked.

"He was riding through here with two white boys in a small Toyota. His ass might still be around here in one of these hoe's houses somewhere. How much money did he steal from shawty?" Charlie asked.

"It wasn't nothing but $1,575, but it's the principle of what he did and who he did it to," Nathan told him.

"Come on, get in y'all, let's go find this nigga," DeWayne said.

They all got in and rode for a couple of minutes around the hood until Charlie seen Neci.

"Pull over right here shawty, so I can ask Neci... Say baby, come here. You seen my cousin, Smooth, around?" he asked from the backseat out the window.

"Yeah, I just seen his high ass acting all strange and shit," she replied.

"Do you know where he is at, baby?" Charlie asked her.

"He's over at Teresa house gettin' high," she told him.

"Ok, baby. Thank you."

They drove a couple of blocks and Charlie pointed the house out as they rode past and let him out.

"Charlie, call Cha-Cha and let her know we found this nigga's ass, while we go back and keep an eye on the house, "Harold told Charlie.

"Gotcha, my nigga," Charlie responded and called right away

Soon as she heard the phone ring, she had it in her hands saying "Hello?"

"Hey, this Charlie. We got Smooth."

"Where that mutherfuckin' bastard at?"

JJ was up and ready to go as soon as he heard those words, with his pistol in one hand and his keys in the other.

"He's over here in Machanicsville, over at Teresa's house getting high."

"I'm on my way," and she hung up the phone, "come on, let's go, they've found that bastard. He's in Machanicsville, over at Teresa's house getting high. That was Charlie. I knew they would find 'em."

Ten minutes later Cha-Cha and JJ pulled up behind DeWayne's car where Smooth was getting high. They all got out of their cars in front of the house with pistols in hand.

"DeWayne, you go around to the backdoor. And if that bastard tries to run---shoot the shit outta his ass. The rest of y'all come with me. Let's go," she said looking around at the group of men who were listening to her every command.

Charlie was the first in line, with Harold beside him since Teresa knew him and she probably would suspect nothing from him. But Smooth was so high that any little movement made him paranoid, and plus he knew that his mama and them would be out looking for him like hell.

KNOCK! KNOCK! KNOCK! KNOCK!

"Who is it?" Teresa asked after a few seconds.

"Open the door, baby. It's me, Charlie."

"Ok, baby give me a second and let me put some clothes on."

Smooth was now getting up telling her, "if he's looking for me, I ain't here, OK?"

"Aight," she said on her way out of the room to open the door.

As soon as the door opened Harold was the first one through the door.

"Bitch, where the fuck is Smooth at, huh?" Harold asked while pointing his pistol in her face.

"He, he, he, he's in the bedroom!" she told him.

As soon as Smooth heard Harold's voice, he was on his way out of the window. He jumped out and took off through the woods as fast as he could. He knew if Harold caught him then he was dead. No question about it.

BOOOOMM! BOOOMM! BOOOOMM! PSS! PSS! PSS! PSS! PSS! PSS!

Harold was shooting his .44 out the window, and DeWayne was shooting at him from behind the house.

"Did anybody hit that bastard? Please tell me one of y'all did," Cha-Cha said as she entered the bedroom where Harold was standing with a smoking gun. DeWayne had made his way around to the window, and was standing on the other side of it.

"Hell naw. I think we missed him. That motherfucka was running like a goddamn cheetah through them woods," Harold said.

"DeWayne, meet us back out front," Cha-Cha said as she and Harold went back into the living-room where everybody else was.

"Bitch, where the fuck he went to?" Harold asked Teresa.

"Man, I don't know. I swear to God," Teresa said, about in tears.

"That's enough! Harold, I don't think she knows," Cha-Cha said, grabbing Harold by the arm, pulling him back and pushing him out the door at the same time.

"Come on, y'all. Let's get the hell outta here. I know somebody done called the police by now," JJ said, heading for the door.

"Look, baby. I'm sorry for having to come over here to your apartment like this, but that bastard stole over $1500 from me," Cha-Cha explained to Teresa.

"Damn, I wish I would've known this at first, Ms. Cha-Cha. I promise, I never would have let him in here," Teresa told her.

"That's ok baby. I know you didn't know, and I'll make sure I get you something back over here for your troubles. Hold on, Charlie, give her $200 for me to have someone fix her window, and I will reimburse you when we get back to the apartment. Here, baby. Here is my number, and all of their numbers too. If you see him, call one of us ASAP," Cha-Cha told her.

"Yes, ma'am I will. I'll be glad to… That motherfucka could've just got me killed for nothing," Teresa said.

"Come on lil lady, it's time to go," Harold called out to Cha-Cha from outside by the car.

"Here I come, right now. Charlie, make sure you give her that money to get that window fixed," she said turning to leave.

Charlie peeled off two one-hundred dollar bills and gave them to her, and assured her that her window would be fixed by that night. Cha-Cha went outside and got back in the car with JJ. They pulled off heading back to Carver Homes to get ready for the get together that night. Deep down, Cha-Cha hoped that at least one of those bullets hit Smooth, so that she could be satisfied a little bit.

"I hope like hell one of them bullets hit that bastard," she told JJ.

"If they did, we'll know in a couple of days," JJ replied and they drove in silence.

Chapter 11

Samantha was sitting out in front of the apartment when everybody else pulled back up. She was sitting in her car when JJ pulled up behind her with her mama on the passenger seat. Then she noticed everyone else pulling up behind JJ. In DeWayne's car with all them together--- it only meant one thing. They've been out looking for her big brother and didn't find 'em, or either they found 'em and fucked him up real bad. No matter what anyone else had thought or said about Smooth, he was her big brother and she loved him dearly. She remembered him before he got on drugs--- he was a very sharp dresser and had it really going on, plus he used to look out for all three of his baby sisters. She sat in her car praying that nothing had happened to her brother, 'cause if it did, it would really break her heart. Plus, she knew the ones who was with her mama were her mama's shooters, and all she had to do was say "kill" and it was done: No matter who it was. They loved her mama so much, sometimes Samantha thought that if Cha-Cha told them to kill themselves, they would do it without question.

"Uh oh. There Samantha go." JJ said as they pulled in behind her.

"I don't give a fuck. I know one goddam thang, she better not come at me talking crazy 'bout that bastard being her big brother or my son." Cha-Cha said.

"Well that's your Samantha, and we all know that. So, I'm going on in the house and let you deal with her. Matter of fact, I'll be back later tonight," JJ told her.

"It ain't shit for me to deal wit! I run this goddam show, not Samantha or anybody else," Cha-Cha reminded him.

Everybody had gotten out of their cars at the same time and Samantha had gotten out of hers, looking crazy at all of'em.

"Where y'all comin from? I hope y'all ain't comin back from hurting my brother or trying to hurt him." Samantha said.

"You don't be questioning nobody, who the hell you thank you is? I run this shit, not you. The bastard shouldn't have stole my muthafuckin' money, and yeah we just comin' back from tryna kill'm! But we missed the bastard!" Cha-Cha told her.

"Nathan! Charlie! That's our brotha, I know y'all ain't tryna hurt him! Please tell me y'all ain't. Harold! You just like our brotha too! Y'all too, DeWayne and JJ, please don't hurt my brotha, please!" Samantha said with sadness in her eyes as they welled up with tears.

"Sis, I'm sorry, but this is our mama, and he violated her bad, so what we s'pose to do?" Nathan asked.

"Shawty, I love'm no doubt, but this lil lady here has raised all of us, and you know like we do, wouldn't nare one of us take a penny from her. So, what gives him the right?" Charlie said.

"Hey baby, you right, but this is mama, and what she say goes." Harold said. DeWayne and JJ just stood there without saying a word.

"He's sick y'all! He needs help! He's sick dammit! Please mama, don't you kill my brotha, please! Mama, have a heart for your flesh and blood , your child, at least for the way he use to be. You know and you haven't forgotten, he's not always been like this mama! He hasn't....He..he..he hasn't mama...Mama, you know it, and he's still a part of you....us, and he needs us more than ever. I feel so weak and nauseas right now, I just wanna throw up...And before y'all were killas, y'all were my brother's brother, and that oughta count for something...Mama..mama..I'm so sick righhh riggghhh...." Samantha threw up and cried so hard that her cries penetrated the walls and ceiling and soared through the clouds as if trying to reach God, pleading with her brother's 'birther' and her mercenaries.

"Oh Lord, somebody help me clean this up..Go get some rags...What am I gonna do with you?! Well child, you better find that bastard, and get 'em some help before we find 'em cause the only help I got for 'em is a bullet to his fuckin head." Cha-Cha told her as Samantha just broke down to her knees still crying as if she were Job and had lost her entire family and all her possessions and will to live, but enduring, managing to eke out, "How can you be so heartless? He's your child, mama! Yours! You had him!" she screeched through the tears and emptiness all doubled over holding her stomach.

Cha-Cha just walked off without even looking back, "And you need to clean yourself up!" Nathan, Harold and Charlie cleaned up the mess and comforted Samantha.

They all just grabbed Samantha, cleaned her up and hugged her while she cried and pleaded for her big brother's life. JJ and DeWayne both just got in their cars and left, because they couldn't stand the sight of seeing Samantha like this. Whether Samantha knew it or not, she was the one who softened every one's hearts toward Smooth that day. All of them really loved her to death and had just about as much respect for her as they had for their mama.

Later on that night when everything and everyone had calmed down, it was time to start getting everything ready for the get together. Samantha and her mama sat together later and had a real serious heart to heart talk. It was groundbreaking that she thought she may have seen her mama soften up just a little, but only time would tell.

"Hey, y'all got that grill ready for this meat yet?" Cha-Cha asked.

"We're out here gettin it ready now baby." Harold said.

"Ok, just let me know when it's ready."

"Ok Mama."

She had about thirty Tie Sticks already rolled up in the bottom of the refrigerator, even though she knew she wouldn't need them all. She also had about twenty cases of Miller ponies and fifty of her pills called "T's". She was expecting anywhere from 30 to 50 people to come through. Then at the end of the night, ain't no telling how many people would show up, because she knew some people from the projects might end up dropping through too.

"The grill ready. What meat you planning cooking first, Mama?"

"Hell, it don't matter. You know you the one who's cooking--- just like always. It's all in here seasoned and ready for you, though."

"Ok Mama."

At first, everything was going as planned concerning the guests, but a few hours later, what was supposed to be a small get together was starting to look like a block party. Cha-Cha had started noticing faces of people she'd never seen before. Her first thought was to clear house, because when you start climbing your way up the ladder in the game, you have to be aware and very careful of unfamiliar faces. So she instantly pulled Harold off of the grill and found Nathan, Charlie, JJ and DeWayne and pulled them all upstairs inside her bedroom for a strategic meeting.

"Look y'all, this little get together is starting to look like a fucking block party, and I ain't feeling this shit at all. It's too many unfamiliar faces. And we all know that can be trouble in the end." Cha-Cha said.

"We can clear this muthafucka out right now if you want us to; all you gotta do is say the word, and it's done. You know that mama." Harold said pulling out his 44 magnum.

"Naw, not just yet. What I do want y'all to do is, Charlie, you stay up here and don't let nobody come up these stairs but one of us. Not even to use the fuckin bathroom."

"Ok Mama."

"Harold, you can go ahead and finish cooking the meat, cause we're goin' to feed them and let 'em get the hell on.

Then I'll choose who leaves and who stays at that point. But if don't either one of us know 'em, they automatically gone."

"Aight, Mama I'm gone back down now then." Harold said.

"JJ, since you're the one who don't drink or smoke, I want you to stay by my side at all times." Cha-Cha told him. He just smiled, because he had read her mind before she even spoke it.

"Here, Nathan I want you to take my pistol, and make sure you stay on point so that means you can't get too fucking drunk or high right now." She said reaching into the closet pulling out her own .357 bulldog passing it to them.

"Here boy, I ain't playing wit you either."

"I know mama, I gotcha," he said as he took the pistol and stood and waited on her to finish talking. Right before she said something to DeWayne, Sheila walked in the room. Nathan, DeWayne, JJ and Charlie all either raised their guns or reached for 'em.

"Girl, you better knock on that goddamn door before you get shot. And why ain't nobody told me my baby was up here anyway?" DeWayne asked.

"I ain't gotta knock on no damn door! This my mama room and if you want me honey, you know how to find me." Sheila responded.

"Ok y'all two love birds can tweet later after we get everything situated. Now like I was saying, DeWayne, do you got your Uzi or your pistol?"

"You know I got the pistol, it's in my hand, but the Uzi is out there in the car."

"Ok, you and Nathan just linger around in the crowd lookin for any suspicious movement, since y'all two know mostly everybody on this side of town. Ok y'all, lets go. Charlie, you won't be up here no longer than two or three hours. It might not be that long, 'cause I'm cleanin this muthafucka out asap. Here's your own personal joint too, and somebody will brang you a plate when you ready for it. " Cha-Cha gave them marching orders.

"Shawty, handle your business. You know I'm strait up here. You know I got this, and I'll be sitting on the steps to make sure don't nobody come up here." Charlie reassured her.

"Ok, come on down here DeWayne; leave that girl alone. Y'all ain't got nut'n but a few more hours. If you want to, hell, brang her down here wit you."

"Naw, she strait up here. I don't wanna have to kill one of these niggas ass about her. Ain't that right?"

"Whatever honey, go on downstairs." Sheila replied.

Chapter 12

Two hours later, all the ribs, chicken, hotdogs and hamburgers was just about done, but enough of it was ready to feed the guests. Plus, he was putting some of it to the side, because they hadn't eaten yet either. Harold thought to himself, "*it's time to feed these muthafuckas and get 'em gone.*" So he went into the living room and turned the music down himself and made the announcement.

"Heeeyyyyyy! Y'all listen up--- time to get yo grub on and get gone! The food is ready, and everyone can get'em a plate, but....but as soon as y'all fix ya plate, I don't know where y'all goin', but y'all gotta get the fuck outta here!!!!! On behalf of Mama Cha-Cha, we thank ya'll for coming out, breakin' bread with us and having' a little fun.

"Damn Harold, you puttin us out already? Shit, the party just getting started good!!" Nose from the next street yelled.

"Naw, not everybody. But Cha-Cha says it's too many new faces here she don't know, plus this was supposed to be a small get together not a fuckin block party. So it's time to clear it out," Harold told him.

"Aight y'all mutherfuckas, let's eat! You heard him. The party's over for all y'all new niggas who we don't know and for some of y'all that we do know." Nose now said, clutching his own pistol.

Cha-Cha was sitting at the table playing spades when she heard Harold make his announcement, so she stopped the card game and got up wit JJ right by her side.

She went to where Harold was standing and said, "Damn Harold, you could've at least gave me a warning that you was about to clear house."

"Warning for what, Mama? You said to feed these niggas' asses and then you wanted your apartment cleared out. So, I'm all about clearing out this damn apartment. If they don't like it, they can get some straitnin, and then we'll shonuff clear house."

"Ok then, handle your business," Cha-Cha told him.

"Yes ma'am. You know I gotchu." Harold replied back.

"You know, that's never been a worry of mines," she told him.

Nose and his brotha Fat was now fixing plates for everybody and telling 'em, "We'll see y'all next time."

They noticed some folks with nasty-ass looks and some was angry, but who cared. Hell, they wasn't from around there, so they could leave in peace or leave in pieces. Either way, it was fine by them, plus they had already noticed DeWayne in his trunk and a couple more of Cha-Cha's people doing the same. So if they knew what was best for them, they'd take their free plates, free liquor, free beer and be happy.

At that point in time, Cha-Cha's husband, Droup, came downstairs clutching a chrome sawed off 12 gauge shotgun in one hand and an Uzi in the other.

As he got to the bottom of the steps, Droup asked, "What the hell is going on down here? 'Cause if you wanna clear this muthafucka out, then I can clear this whole goddamn apartment and yard by my damn self!!!!!"

He had been upstairs all night since he had come in from work. Honestly, he was already kind of pissed off, because he didn't know anything about the get together or the money that was stolen until he got home. The only people who could control him when he was angry or upset were his daughters and his wife, no one else. But tonight, wasn't nobody gonna be able to control him.

"Ooooohhhhhh shit, goddammit." Everyone said when they saw him at the bottom of the steps wit guns in both hands. "We got it Droup." Harold said wit a smile on his face, because he knew he was looking at a quiet killa who very seldom got angry.

"Daddy!!!! Go on back upstairs wit them. Everything's Ok" Samantha and Sheila said while trying to hug their daddy, but it wasn't working tonight.

"I ain't going no goddamn where! Now move out of my goddamn way!!!!" Droup demanded.

The girls immediately moved out of his way as he walked through the living room on his way to the kitchen where his wife was playing spades. Nobody in the kitchen or at the card table said anything except, "Wassup Droup." He just stood there looking crazy for a while at first, then he finally said, "Ain't nut'n." Then he turned and went back upstairs.

After they cleared out the party, and everything was finally calm, they locked the front door. Now it was just family and a few friends whom Cha-Cha knew she could trust. Harold was still on the back porch grilling the steaks and the rest of the chicken. At that point they continued to have their own lil' private get together that went on until about three or four o'clock in the morning.

The next morning, Cha-Cha woke up to Punkin giving her the phone.

"Mama, mama get up!" Punkin told her, "someone's on the telephone."

"Boy, who is it?" she asked him, "see what the hell they want. Shit, can't you see I'm trying to sleep."

"She said, who is it? She's trying to sleep." Punkin said into the phone, then he listened to the response. "Ok hold on. Mama it's Tyrone. He said you need to get on the phone."

"Hand it here. Hello?" Cha-Cha said, still half asleep as she tried to listen. "Ok, matter of fact what time is it? Two o'clock? Damn, I need to get my ass up anyway." He must have asked her what the hell they did last night , 'cause she went to explaining and apologizing at the same time.

"I had a lil get together last night. Ok, I'll make sure I invite you next time, I promise. Ok, I'll see you in a few."

She got on up, noticing Punkin still standing there by her bed side, listening and watching her the whole time.

"Boy where's everybody at?" she asked him.

"I don't know, I guess they all gone, except for Nathan, he's still downstairs sleep."

"Go wake him up, and tell'm I said Tyrone is on the way over here. How long have you been up, and where's my baby, Enos at? Have y'all ate?"

"Yes ma'am, we ate some barbecue. Enos in my room watching TV," Punkin said on his way downstairs to wake up Nathan.

Everyone was now up in the apartment and sitting in the living room when Tyrone pulled up. He brought two big brown grocery sacks in wit'm this time. Cha-Cha met him at the door to let him in.

"Hey baby, it sho looks like Christmas done arrived early for me," Cha-Cha said as he came in.

"Yeah, I guess you can say that. This right here is the last of what I got, and if anybody goin to get it, I'd rather for it to be you," he said, heading on into the living room, smiling.

"You sho know how to make me feel special, don't you? Tell me how long you go'n be out of this shit, so I can know what I need to do?" Cha-Cha asked him.

"You know you're special baby, and since I'm 'bout to take me a trip wit some of my people, I might be gone for a month or two," Tyrone told her.

"A month or two! What the fuck you tryin' to do nigga, starve me to death?" Cha-Cha said, looking shocked.

"Naw, baby I ain't trying to starve you to death. That's why I'm bringing you my last thirty pounds I got left, so you can create your own prices and create you a drought. I still got you two more bags out there in my car," Tyrone explained.

"Ok baby, sounds good to me, but damn I gotta make sure I pace this and stretch it out. Nathan, go get them other two bags outta his car for me."

"K."

"Punkin, wassup my main man? I see your mama got you around learning all you can, huh? It won't be long before you're ready to start selling your own at the rate you're learning." Tyrone said, giving Punkin a high five.

"Wassup Tyrone?! Yeah, you know, I gotta learn all I can so when it's time, I can start helping you and my mama move y'all weed," Punkin responded.

"You ain't got nothin' but a few more years before you're ready, so just be patient, because it's comin," Tyrone told him.

"Ok"

"Punkin, gone on upstairs and take Enos with you; we'll handle this later. But right now, I got some real business to handle," Cha-Cha said as Nathan was coming back in the front door with two more big brown sacks in his hands.

"Yes ma'am! See ya later, Tyrone," Punkin said while heading upstairs with Enos to watch TV.

Chapter 13

Now Tyrone, Cha-Cha, and Nathan were sitting downstairs in the living room with thirty pounds of Tie Stick sitting in front of them in four grocery bags.

"When you planning on goin outta town?" Cha-Cha asked, she added, "I gotta get you your money. If I calculate this right, I owe you $36,000 for this thirty right?"

"We should be leaving Monday morning, because he wants me to take a look at a new batch of shit that he's getting. Plus we're going to look at some property he's thinking about buying overseas. He wants me to go in wit him on the property so we can start growing our own weed. So you know what that means for you. You'd have more weed than you could ever sell, and more money than you can hide," Tyrone told her. Cha-Cha's eyes lit up at the thought of all that money.

Tyrone continued, "Also in the process, we're taking a vacation, so I'm looking to be gone no longer than two months but I might be back before then. Speaking of the price for these pounds… I'm not charging you no damn $36,000 for this shit. For you, just give me $20,000 for'em so that should mean by the time I get back I will be able to sell you at least a hundred pounds of this shit."

"$20,000!!!" She said with nothing but dollar signs in her eyes. She knew the type of money she was about to make now, especially when she created a drought on this weed.

"Hold on! I'll be right back. I'm about to pay you your money right goddamn now," she told Tyrone.

Already on her feet, she headed upstairs to her secret stash spot, that nobody else knew about. One day, a few weeks back, when she was at home alone, she had her personal maintenance man, Mr. Hickerson, come over and build a secret spot in the ceiling of Punkin's bedroom closet. Inside of it, she hid over $40,000 that only she knew about.

First, she went inside her own closet and reached into her husband's long leather French coat and grabbed the $6,000 she hid in there. Then she headed to Punkin's bedroom.

She walked into the room and told them, "Punkin, you and Enos go in my room for a quick second, so I can handle something in here."

"Yes ma'am. Come on lil brotha, let's go in mama room so she can handle something right quick."

Punkin grabbed Enos by the hand and they left, heading into their mama's room.

Once they were in her room, Cha-Cha closed and locked the door. She then grabbed the milk crate she had in there, and brought it into the closet. She carefully climbed on top of the crate. Reaching up, she pushed open the secret spot, then grabbed the big box marked 'steel toe boots.'

Cha-Cha climbed back down and sat on Punkin's bed. She counted out $14,000 more to go with the $6,000 in her pocket. She kept the money in bundles of $10,000, but inside of each $10,000 bundle, she had 5 smaller bundles, each with $2,000, so it would always be a quick count. Luckily for her, she always thought ahead.

On her way back downstairs, she started to formulate a plan. Since she had already been out of weed for two whole days, she could prolong it for about two whole weeks. It was time for her to create her own drought. She knew instead of charging $200 an ounce, she could start charging anywhere from $350 to about $450 an ounce, depending on how bad the streets wanted it. Once she made this deal with Tyrone, she'd have 38 pounds total. Plus, out of 38 pounds, she would have 608 ounces to sell at **her** price. At whatever price she decided to sell it, she was looking at no less than over $200,000 to a quarter of a million dollars cash. But depending on the fluctuation of the prices she might see over a quarter of a million and all she was paying for it was $20,000. They always say "stay down till you come up." Well, she was about to come up and over the top with this one. She then walked back into the living room.

"Here baby, here's all of your money. So, you won't have to wait on it; you know I like handling my business." She said, handing him rolls of cash in rubber bands that surprised everyone.

Nathan's eyes grew big as hell when he saw the rolls of cash. He knew she had some money put up for a rainy day, but he never would've thought she had $20,000 in cash right here in this apartment.

"Damn baby! You know I ain't in no hurry for this money," Tyrone told Cha-Cha, "but it is just like you to wanna go ahead and get it out of the way and not have anything hangin' over your head. Listen, you know you don't need to be having this type of money around in this apartment. I understand that people respect you and know you got a team of killas, but money will make even your closest friends turn on you baby. Ok? You know, I'm telling you this, because I love you girl," Tyrone said in all seriousness.

"Ok baby. I know you do, and you damn sho right about what money will make people do. I've been thinking about moving anyway or getting me a stash house just so I can stash my shit there, but I haven't really had enough for that. But if everything goes well with this…The way I'm planning it to go, then I will be able to do what I need to do."

"Now that's using your head and just in case you do move… Never keep all of your money in the apartment! Always keep just enough to handle what you need handled. Like they say: 'Never put all your eggs in one basket,'" Tyrone added.

"And that's so true," Cha-Cha said, "thank you sugga."

They sat around talking a little while longer. Before long, Tyrone got up to go and gave her a hug and shook Nathan's hand. He had been noticing the dollar signs in her eyes when he gave her the price for the weed, and that's exactly what he wanted to see. One thing he knew, when he got back, she'd be well over the top.

After Tyrone left, she and Nathan took all four of the grocery bags upstairs to her bedroom where Enos and Punkin were still sitting. They dumped all 30 pounds out on the bed. Punkin and Enos's eyes got big as quarters when they saw all the weed their mama had just exposed them to.

"Mama, we finna git wich ain' we?" Enos asked.

"Mama finna try to get us rich baby," Cha-Cha told him.

"O'tay."

"Man, mama that's a whole lot of weed. You gon' give me some?" Punkin asked.

"Naw, baby. Not just yet, you gotta few more years to go. Alright?" Cha-Cha told him.

"Yes ma'am."

"You ready now lil girl! You can start doing you shonuff now mama; I know you 'bout to sell these pounds ASAP." Nathan said.

"No the hell I ain't. Did you hear what Tyrone just said? He's goin' to be gone for probably two months. These thirty pounds is the last of the weed left. So, I would be a damn fool to not create a drought and jack the prices up to damn near double. So, I ain't moving shit for at least two or three weeks at the most. Then watch how fast it goes and how bad they're goin' to want it," she said, trying to help him understand the bigger picture.

"This is a lot of weed to break down in ounces to sell, mama. But I get the picture... Since you're the only one wit it for sale, stall the streets out for a while to make'em fiend like heroin junkies, then feed'em wit they medication. Then stall them again and again. So by the time Tyrone do get back, you'd be able to sell at least fifty to a hundred pounds in about a week," Nathan said, with dollar signs in his eyes.

"Now you're starting to think like a hustler. The way I've been trying to get you to think forever, knuckle-head, but watch me on this move, and make sure you learn. This right here will take me over the top, guaranteed," Cha-Cha said, with a gleam in her eye.

"Ok lil girl, you're the mama and the boss, or should I say the teacher?" Nathan asked.

"Momma and teacher sounds better," she replied, while they both just smiled at each other.

"Come on, enough talking. We gotta get this shit wrapped up and shipped out of here until I get ready for it. Plus, I gotta call Samantha so she can come and get this shit and put it up," Cha-Cha said.

Next, she was on the phone calling Samantha to come back over to the apartment. Cha-Cha had bought Samantha an extra refrigerator just for this purpose. She also planned to have Samantha buy a thick chain and a master lock so nobody else could get into it but them. No one else knew she was keepin it at Samantha's anyway, because when it came to secrets--- she was a lady of many.

"Hello?" Samantha answered.

"Hey lil girl, what you doin? I need you to come back over here real quick and see me. I got something for you," Cha-Cha told her.

"Ok, I'll be there in a few."

"Ok see you then."

It only took Samantha twenty minutes to get over there after she hung up the phone. When she got there, she used her key to let herself in and headed straight upstairs to where she knew her mama would be. As soon as she got upstairs to her mama's room, she was so surprised to see so much weed sitting on her mama's bed.

"Man, mama how much weed that is? 'Cause from what I see, it looks about like a hundred pounds." Samantha said.

"Girl naw, it ain't nothin' but thirty, and I need for you to take it wit you and put it up for two or three weeks for me," Cha-Cha told her.

"Dat's a lot of weed you want me to hold onto."

"What the hell is you scared of? Don't nobody else know you got it but us. Don't you start that scary shit on me, girl."

"Scared? I ain't scared of nothin."

"A'ight then. So, don't be fucking acting like it then. I got real big plans for all of this anyway. It's going to take me over the top when I'm done with it. Tyrone, my weed man, will be gone out of town for a month or two, and this all the weed that I got to last me. I also got some money I'm going to need you to hold for me too, until I find somewhere else to put it. Hold on, I'll be right back," Cha-Cha said.

She then got up and went into Punkin's room again and sent them back into her room and went in the closet and grabbed her shoe box again. She put it under her arm and went back into her room. When she opened up the shoe box everybody's eyes got big as hell. Punkin and Enos started trying to grab the money.

"Move them hands back," she told them.

They moved their hands, then the only thing you heard was "Gimme, gimme, gimme."

Then Cha-Cha told them, "Gimme is what got all y'all ass here." Now all y'all hold on. That's why y'all ain't never knew I had any money.

"How much money is that anyway mama?" Samantha asked.

"It should be about $26,000 left in here. It was $40,000 until I just pulled out $14,000 to go with my other $6,000 to make up the $20,000 I had to give Tyrone for these 30 pounds right here. Don't worry about it girl, I'm going to pay you good for holding my shit. And I need to recount it anyway, just to make sure what it is," Cha-Cha told her.

She then recounted it, and when she had finished, she had counted $28,000! That was $2,000 more than what she had expected. She then gave Samantha $20,000 to take and put up for her. Then she gave Samantha $2,500 and took out $500 more and split it up between Enos and Punkin. She looked at Nathan, standing there smiling, and gave him a one-dollar bill. Everybody in the room started laughing.

"Boy, you know I'm just playing witchu."

Then she gave him $1,000 for himself, which left her with $4,000. She thought she would surprise her husband by giving him $3,000. After all, he did deserve it, and she would only keep $1,000 for herself.

After she finished giving everyone their money, every one of them hugged her neck, and told her they loved her and thanked her. She knew that every last one of them truly meant what they said, but they had no idea that what she had just done was just the beginning of what she truly had in store for her family.

Nathan got up and went downstairs, and when he had returned, he had a big red cooler and two bags of ice. He took the two bags of ice into the bathroom and crushed them up fine in the tube then turned back to the room and put a thin layer of ice in the bottom of the cooler. He then took the pounds and put them in the bottom of the cooler. He was able to work 15 pounds in the bottom, then he put another thin layer of ice on them and stacked the last 15 pounds in the cooler. After having all 30 pounds inside the cooler, he took the rest of the ice and poured it inside to cover up the exposed foil, then he closed the top. The whole time he was doing it, Punkin was right by his side looking at what he was doing. Samantha then grabbed the $20,000, put it inside of one of her mama's purses, then zipped it up. She and Nathan were headed out the back door, but she turned around at the door.

"Mama, all this money you got, and you wanna kill my brotha over 1500 dollars? You just gave me that and more, myself. Then between Nathan, Punkin, and Enos, you just about gave them that all except for maybe $75. I can't understand it for the life of me. Yeah, he stole your money, but he's sick Mama."

"I don't give a fuck how sick he is and how much money I got. None of that matters. What matters is that the bastard stole my fuckin' money. Now you better go on and leave it alone before I start back looking for him to kill his ass. Naw, hold on before you go, answer this question. Would you steal from me?"

"Mama, you know I wouldn't steal from you."

"Ok then what in the fuck gives him the right? Fuck that 'he sick' shit, he still knows right from goddamn wrong. Now gone, 'cause I'm gettin' pissed the fuck off."

Samantha just looked at her mama and shook her head. She just left, because she knew, as of right now, she wasn't gettin' through to her mama, but she hoped she would be able to one day. Then she and Nathan went on outside. After he put the cooler in her trunk, she just looked at him.

"Nathan, please don't let mama hurt Smooth! If y'all get word of 'em, please call me so I can go get'm and try to get him some help. I'll pay her back her money. I love my brotha, and deep down inside, he really means well! I know he do, he's just sick right now," Samantha petitioned for her brother.

"Look, you're asking me to go against mama for you girl. I love you, and I have a lot of respect for you! But understand, that's our mama, and if she knew we was even having this conversation, she'd cut us off or kill us. I'm going to do it this time, but don't ever ask me to do nothing else like this again lil girl. You better call Harold, JJ, DeWayne and Charlie and ask them the same thang. Honestly though, I do think you've change her mind a little bit, 'cause she ain't mentioned it since y'all two talked."

"Ok, thank you big brotha! I love you, and I'll make sure I call the rest of 'em soon as I get home," Samantha told him.

"I love you too, lil sis."

After hugging each other, she left and he went back inside.

Chapter 14

A full week hadn't even passed yet, and her phone just rang off the hook. Everybody was looking for some Tie Stick, and she kept telling them the same thing---that she was waiting on it, and that it was a drought right now. She knew she wouldn't be able to hold out for a full three weeks, but she would make it to two weeks though. After about ten days, she called Samantha and told her she was coming down there to pick up 10 pounds so she could start getting them ready. After she picked them up, she went back home and spent a whole day breaking them down to nothing but ounces. She knew she would sell them for no less than $350 apiece. By this time, the streets were going crazy for it. Nobody wanted to smoke or sell anything else but Tie Stick, because of the high and the money.

By the fourteenth day, she had put her plan into motion. She started making calls telling everyone the same thing.

All she had to say was, "Hey baby, I just found some, and it's not that much, and you know it's a drought. They charging me an arm and a leg for this shit. So, I gotta have

$350 an ounce. Unfortunately, I'm not gonna be able to do any deals, period."

And just like she expected, nobody complained about the price. They just wanted the product. Even though she had 160 ounces for sale, she consistently told them she only had a few left. Within three days, she had moved the whole 160 ounces at $350 apiece. So, in three days, she had made $56,000 dollars! And she still had 28 more pounds left to sell.

That 28 pounds, she was going to stretch out to last for another month and a half. When she called Samantha in 3 days, she told her she needed to talk to her and Droup and that they would come by that night. Neither Samantha nor Droup had any idea of what they were about to hear. Her husband knew his wife was hustling and just had given him $3,000 a few weeks ago, but he had no idea how much weed she was buying or how much money she was making.

Later that night, Cha-Cha told Droup she needed to talk to him and Samantha down at Samantha's apartment. Cha-Cha, Droup, Enos, and Punkin all got into their light blue LTD Ford with tinted windows and headed down to Samantha's apartment. Cha-Cha had $56,000 in her purse that Droup was clueless about. A few minutes later, they pulled up in front of their daughter's apartment, got out, and locked the doors. "*It's not time to reveal everything to my family*," Cha-Cha thought as they headed into Samantha's apartment.

"Punkin and Enos, ya'll two go into Samantha's room and watch some TV for a while. I need to talk to Samantha and y'all Daddy," Cha-Cha told them.

"Yes, ma'am. Come on lil brotha, let's go in big sister's room, and watch some TV," Punkin said, taking Enos's hand and leading him out of the room.

"Ok, now what I want to talk about might shock y'all," Cha-Cha said and then continued," Samantha, you already know a little bit, but not all of it. Droup you don't know none of it, so just hear me out first," she told him.

"Ya'll know I been hustling, but don't either of you know to what extent I've *really* been hustlin'. In this purse is $56,000 dollars, and I made it all in three days. Well, it didn't even take a full three days, more like two and a half. Droup, Samantha is already holding $20,000 that I gave to her to put up a few weeks ago. Plus, she got 28 pounds that I gave her at the same time as the money. Before Tyrone went out of town, he sold me nearly 30 pounds for $20,000. He's the only one with this kind of reefer, Tie Stick, and he sold me the rest of what he had. So, now I'm the only person in Atlanta with it, Period! I've created a drought, and the streets out there is going crazy for it. So by the time I finish sellin' the rest of it,

I should have made anywhere from $200,000 to $250,000, if not more!" she said, and then paused as she saw the dollar signs in their eyes.

After giving them a moment to process what she said, Cha-Cha continued with her plan.

"So, listen. I'm about to buy us a house on my next shipment, since I would have enough money to get it. I'd just be using the apartment strictly for selling weed. I don't trust the bank, so Samantha will be holding on to all the money until I find somewhere else to stash it safely. All of our hard times and struggles end here and now, unless something goes wrong, of course. I been having Nathan groom Punkin for the streets. That is who I want to take over after me. Now you know why he was with me sackin up weed, 'Mr. Man'. I know you got something to say, so go ahead and get it out now," she articulated.

"How you know I want my goddamn son selling that shit? Hell, there's already enough of y'all sellin' it. I want him to make something out of his damn self, not end up in chain gang," Droup told her.

"Look, I see it in him. He's around me all day every day looking and learning while you're at work. He's too damn curious," Cha-Cha explained to Droup.

"Ok, since you wanna make him a goddamn dope dealer, he better not call me if his ass goes to jail," Droup told her.

"Man, shut up. You talkin' stupid. Cause if he do go--- you go'n go get 'em, and if you don't, I will. You got anything to say Samantha?" Cha-Cha asked, looking at her daughter.

"Naw, Mama. Just be careful, and let's get rich," Samantha told her.

"I'm damn sho tryin' baby!" Cha-Cha told her.

After their discussion, Cha-Cha recounted her money and gave Samantha $50,000 to put up with the $20,000, so she would have $70,000 already put up. Then she counted out $2,000 and gave it to Samantha. She told Samantha she would be calling her again in a few weeks for some more weed. She told her it would probably be 10 pounds worth this time around as well.

On the way home, later that evening, what Cha-Cha said hit Droup full force.

"You mean to tell me you been selling all this goddamn shit, and I've still been giving you all my check? Why in the hell you just now tellin me this shit? I should've been the first to know," he said with disappointment evident in his voice.

"You know....you right! I should've been done told you about what I was doing. But you know now, and you can start keeping all your money. But it ain't like I was fucking it up. Hell, it's part of that $20,000 that Samantha was holding the first time. I'll be sure to let you know from now on, Mr. Man," she committed to Droup.

Turning to the kids in the back seat, she asked, "Ya'll want something to eat?"

"Yes, ma'am," they both responded at once.

"What y'all want to eat? Some fish from Fish Supreme or some hot wings from the Plaza?" she asked them.

"Both," Punkin said.

"Well, y'all ain't getting no goddamn both, so which one you want?" Droup asked.

"Don't you be fucking cursing at him like you crazy. Every time you say something to him, you always gotta curse at him. Well, he ain't no goddamn dog, and you ain't gonna keep cursing at him. And if he wants both, he'll fucking get both. Now stop, so I can get their food," Cha-Cha told Droup.

"You ain't gonna be satisfied 'til I lock your goddamn jaws, now keep on!" Droup said.

"The day you put your goddamn hands on me, that'll be the day I bury your stankin-ass, nigga," she told him.

Droup just looked at her, because he knew, just like she knew, he would never hit her, and if he did, it we be because she would have seriously crossed a line in the sand whereas she had violated him in such a heinous way that she deserved to die, and he would probably kill her. That was unlikely to happen, though. No matter what little or big shit they went through, he loved his wife to death, and she loved him.

When they stopped on Pryor Rd to get the hot wings, people approached her from all directions asking when the next time was that she would be straight. The only thing she said was that she was still waiting to hear something else in about another week, or maybe before.

This was one of Droup's favorite hangout spots, because just about all of his drinking buddies were there, and he knew there would be something good to drink there. So while Cha-Cha and the kids went in the café to order the food, Droup went to where his buddies were and tossed back a few bottles.

"Punkin, go out there and see what your damn daddy is doing," Cha-Cha said and added "I bet his ass is out there getting drunk with them damn niggas. If he is, tell him I said don't get drunk, because he know he gotta drive us home."

"Yes, ma'am," Punkin replied.

Punkin went back out of the café in search of his daddy, and he didn't have to look very far. His daddy was on the other end of the plaza with about six or seven of his drinking buddies, just like his mama said he would be. Punkin recognized a few of them from when they had come to their apartment. He saw one arm Rick, Nose, Hot Pocket, Jack in the wheelchair, and a couple more who he didn't know. But for some reason, they all seemed to know who he was.

"Here comes your son, Droup," one arm Rick said, "Wassup, Punkin?"

"Nothing, wassup Rick?" Punkin mildly replied.

Then everybody started speaking to Punkin while his daddy just stood there. One thing Punkin hated about this end of the plaza was that it smelled like old piss, and there were a lot of wine bottles and drunk people all over.

"I guess your ma sent you out here to see what the hell I'm doing, huh?" Droup asked.

"She just told me to come out here and see if you was out here getting drunk, and if you was, to tell you don't drink too much, because you still gotta drive us home," Punkin told him.

"Go in there and tell your ma I said I know what the hell I gotta do!"

"Yes, sir!" Punkin responded.

But before Punkin left, all of them said, "Cha-Cha in there? Why you ain't tell us she was up here with you? Where she at Punkin?"

"She's in the café waiting on our food," Punkin told them.

Not even a full second after the words left the tip of his tongue, all of'em jumped up scurrying to get to Cha-Cha and left Droup standing there by himself holding a bottle. Everyone really did love Cha-Cha. Punkin was in hot pursuit to see what they wanted with his mama.

"Hey Cha-Cha! Hey girl! Hey baby! Wass up sugga!" was all the cafe' occupants heard as they entered the café, hugging on Cha-Cha showing her some love.

"Hey y'all, wassup!" a surprised Cha-Cha excitedly responded as they entered.

"Why you didn't let nobody know you was up here? You know we all gotta keep an eye on you and protect you baby," Nose told her.

"I wish a mothafucka would try and mess wit Cha-Cha. I'll come up out this mothafuckin' wheelchair on they ass!" Jack said.

"Ain't nobody stupid enough to fuck wit her. That's my baby, ain't that right, sugga!" Hot Pocket said.

"A nigga fuck wit Cha-Cha?!! Whaaat? I be on his ass like I got two arms," one arm Rick said, doing a quick shuffle with his feet and his one arm. They died laughing!

"Y'all know I got my lil friend with me, and y'all know I'll use him," Cha-Cha said, patting her side where her gun was tucked into her waistband. Then she asked, "What y'all doing here besides gettin' drunk?"

"Waiting on you to give us one of them good ass joints, that Tie Stick reefer you got," Hot Pocket said, and everybody else added in, "Hell yeah, baby we need us one."

Cha-Cha reached in her bra and came out with her cigarette pack and gave them one. She also gave Hot Pocket a hundred-dollar bill and told him to go to Fish Supreme, across the street and order a hundred pieces of fish, hush puppies, some fries, and some coleslaw.

"Mama, can I go with Hot Pocket?" Punkin asked.

"Come on, boy. You don't have to ask her to come. Come on let's go! "Hot Pocket said.

As they turned and got ready to leave Cha-Cha said, "Hot!"

"Yeah, sugga."

"That fish and stuff is for y'all to eat, and y'all can drink up the rest of the change, I don't care. But you better make sure all y'all get some, if not, then I'm coming back up here and whoop some ass, now. You know I'ma find out. I want 6 pieces of fish for my babies to eat."

"Ok, baby. And you know whatever you say gets done, just like you say."

"I'll be over there as soon as these wings get ready," Cha-Cha told him.

"We'll be there," Hot Pocket told her.

Everyone else who was left in the café starting to thank Cha-Cha, telling her how sweet she was, how much they loved her, and how she was the only person who would think to do the things she did for people. Droup stood there the whole time. He knew that everyone from Carver Homes, Joyland, High Point, Lakewood Village, and the plaza loved his wife. There wasn't anything he could do about it. She was just one of those people that people loved. But if you crossed her, you'd have hell to pay, and they all knew that.

A few minutes after Hot Pocket and Punkin left the café, Cha-Cha's wings were ready. She said her goodbyes and promised to have another get together for everyone real soon. Droup and Cha-Cha got in the car and drove across the street to Fish Supreme and waited on Hot Pocket to come out with the fish. A few minutes later, Punkin and Hot Pocket came out with a box of fish, which Hot Pocket handed to Cha-Cha as Punkin got in the backseat.

"I told them to get ten pieces ready real quick, and I'll wait on the other ninety pieces. You know we can't have you out here in the streets too late. A'ight Droup, see you later. Take care of our baby. I would hate to have to come see about you," Hot Pocket told Droup.

Droup just laughed and replied, "Ok Hot, I gotcha."

"Later Punkin and Enos," Hotpocket said to the boys in the backseat.

"Later!" said the boys.

Sheila was standing in the doorway when they pulled back up to the apartment, looking like she was so glad to see them get back home.

"Wherever y'all been, this phone hasn't stopped ringing since I walked through the front door. You got about 30 messages and, should I say, people who said call them. What is that y'all got to eat?" Sheila asked.

"Hell, they can wait. Did Tyrone call?" Cha-Cha asked.

"Yeah, he did. He said to tell you he'll be back in another five or six more weeks. Y'all bring some food home? Cause I sho do smell some hot wings and fish," Sheila said.

"Here big susta," Enos said, handing her the food.

"Good," Cha-Cha said. That's exactly what she wanted to hear. She needed him to be gone for a good while longer so she could finish out her plans with her drought.

Chapter 15

It had been three weeks since Smooth had stolen his mama's money. He knew unless God was with him when she caught up with him, he was a dead man. He had no idea how he had escaped the day he did, because a flurry of bullets had flown past his head as he ran through the woods. Some of them came so close that they grazed his clothes. When he realized the shooting had ceased and there wasn't anyone chasing after him, he stopped and stripped down to check himself to make sure he hadn't been hit. To his surprise, they missed his flesh completely. He hadn't taken a full bath in weeks, just a wash up here and there and he was barely even eating. One thing he knew for certain was that he couldn't let his mama find out where he was. Even when he wasn't high, he was still paranoid. He had made a mistake that day by letting Charlie see him and talk to him, but that was a mistake he wouldn't make again.

To make it even worse, the money he stole didn't even last him a whole week. It might have lasted him four days at the most, and he couldn't even enjoy it in peace. He was thinking, at any moment, Cha-Cha was going to burst in with Harold and the rest of them, and this time, he would be dead meat for sure, six feet and pushing up daisies. One thing he knew, his odds of living much longer were very slim, because, likely, one time or another, time wasn't on his side...he was a dead man walking one way or another, and he had no idea who could save him. On days when he wasn't getting high, he thought of the fucked up shit he had done, and it hurt to think about it. But he felt like it was too late to turn back, so he just kept getting high to ease his conscience.

He often thought about his sisters, Samantha, Sheila, and Baby Girl, because at one point he had been very close to them. He used to take care of them when they were small before he was on drugs. He knew only one of them his mama couldn't stand beside him; that was Baby Girl, because she and their mama were too much alike. But he didn't know where he could find her or if she knew what he had done. He seriously doubted she knew, because his mama barely trusted Baby Girl. The problem was that Baby Girl was always around JJ, and Smooth knew that JJ would kill or at least shoot him on sight. In fact, Smooth was sure that his mama had given all of them the order to do just that, shoot him dead on sight, so calling Baby Girl was out.

When Smooth thought about it, he practically couldn't go anywhere on the side of town where she lived. It would be complete suicide. She had been running them streets over there since she was a lil girl, and she knew damn near everybody in the area. Plus now, she was hustling and not drinking anymore; those two things made her known by even more people. But Smooth was desperate, so one day he couldn't take it anymore and decided to take a chance by calling Samantha.

RING! RING! RING!

"Hello?"

"Hey lil sis"

"WHO IS THIS?" Samantha yelled in to the phone, hoping it was her brother.

"This your brother, girl!"

"SMOOTH?" an elated Samantha asked.

"Yeah, it's me," he told her.

"BOY, WHERE THE HELL YOU AT?!!!??!! I've been over here worried sick about your ass. I didn't know if Mama and them had done shot and killed you or what! I been begging Mama not to kill you if she found you and telling her all type of shit to keep yo' ass alive!! Smooth, what the hell was you thinking stealing from our mama, anyway? What the hell is wrong with you?" Samantha unloaded.

Smooth was so glad to hear that his lil sister, Samantha, was so concerned about him that he started crying. He knew no matter what he did, she was the one he could depend on to have his back. It felt good to know, but at the same time it hurt like hell.

"I don't know what got in to me that day. I was high on that shit, and I needed some money. I didn't mean to take that much from her though, and I hate that I did it, because they almost killed me. If there wasn't a God in heaven watching over me, I know I'd be dead as hell right now," he told her.

"Do you know that money you stole from Mama was nothing? She's been giving that type of money away, boy. Since you've done that, I can't count how much money she has given away. Like I said, it isn't the money she's mad about, it's the principle of the thing. You supposed to be her son, and you go and steal from her. That's what's got her so goddamn mad. And nigga, she is mad too! But where is you at, so I can come and get you. I can't bring you back to my apartment, because ain't no telling when she'll pop up," Samantha told him.

"I'm over here by Techwood projects where I've been staying on the streets and sleeping in cars. You ain't trying to set me up is you sis?" he asked her.

"Boy if you don't stop talking stupid! Now where exactly is you at?" she asked.

Smooth told her exactly where he was, and she was there within 30 minutes. When she pulled up and saw him, he looked and smelled so bad, but she didn't care. She grabbed him and hugged him while she cried, because she was just so happy he was safe. They got in her car and went and bought him some clothes, shoes, underwear, and socks. She then took him to get a haircut, some eats, and to get a hotel room for a month. She wanted to know that her big brother would have somewhere to lay his head at night. The room had a small refrigerator and a small kitchen so that he could prepare himself something to eat, but Smooth couldn't boil water. So, Samantha told him she would come by every few days to feed him and give him some spending money until their mama's anger blew over. But who knew how long that would be, because once you got her mad, she held a grudge for a very long time. She also told him she was going to pay the money back to their mama for him in small amounts so she could act like it was coming from him. She assured him that he would be safe if he stayed in Forrest Park where she had him now, keeping him out of harm's way.

Samantha stayed with Smooth while he showered and got freshened up. When he came out of the bathroom, she just sat and looked at him, because now he was looking more like the big brotha she once knew. She knew he was still hungry, so she went up the street to Zesto's and bought him something else to eat. By the time she got back to the hotel, he was on the bed half asleep. She gave him the food and watched him eat it while he was nodding off. The next thing she knew, he was out. So, she turned off the light and put the rest of the food back in the wrapper so he would have it for later.

Before she left, she put a hundred-dollar bill on the side table and a note telling him not to buy any drugs with the money. She knew in her gut that she should not have left any money, because she knew he would use it to on drugs. She locked the room up and left so he could get some rest.

Smooth slept for three days straight! He only got up when he had to use the bathroom, and then he went right back to sleep. Samantha was so surprised when she went back over there three days later to find Smooth still asleep. She had to beat on the door to get him to wake up. When he finally came to the door, still half asleep, she handed him two plates she had cooked for him. When he took the tin foil off the plates and saw Ox Tail, collard greens, cornbread, macaroni and cheese, rice, and even some fried chicken, he immediately sat down and started eating cave man style like he had no manners at all. It had been so long since he had eaten a good home-cooked meal that he ate so fast, Samantha thought he was going to choke on the food. He barely came up for air, the food was so good. Finally, when he was full and about done, talking with food in his mouth, he said, "Mmmm thank you lil sis, this shit here is so damn good. You know it's been a long time since I had a good home-cooked meal!"

"You're welcome, big brother! I see you haven't touched the money or the note I left for you," she told him.

"What money and what note?" He asked.

Then he finally looked on the table beside his bed and saw five twenty-dollar bills and a note.

"Hell, I've been asleep, and I ain't noticed nothin'. Matter of fact, how long have I been asleep anyway?"

"Three days, boy. Your ass been sleep for three whole days!" Samantha told him.

"Damn! Have you seen Mama or talked to her?" he asked.

"Naw, I been too scared to go over there. She might be able to tell I been around you. You know how Mama got her instincts about all of her kids," Samantha told him.

"Yeah, I know, right! It's scary, because that lady know all of us like a book!"

"She damn sho do! But I gotta get back home, just in case she calls. Bruh, start taking better care of yourself, please. And I will see you in a few days," she reminded him.

"Ok, lil sis, I will!" he told her.

"Come and give me a hug, boy! I love you big bro!"

"I love you too lil sis, and thank you so much for being here for me!"

"Boy, go on with that! You ain't gotta thank me. I remember when you use to take care of me, so it's the least I can do for you now," she said handing him another one hundred-dollar bill.

"Here. This is for you too. I know you're going to get high, but get you some food too, just in case I don't make it back in 3 days," she told him.

"Ok, lil sis."

As Samantha drove home, she kept thinking about Smooth. She wondered how long it would take him to get rid of his drug habit. She knew no matter what, she would never turn her back on her brother. She also knew she had to find a way to get their mama to forgive him, even though that would be the hardest part of all. Samantha prayed that one day her mama would eventually be able to forgive Smooth. But for now, Samantha would do all she could to help him and make sure her mama stayed in the dark about it.

Chapter 16

It had been a whole week since Cha-Cha sold any weed and people wanted it bad, way more than before, craaazy! She didn't know what Tyrone had on the reefer she was getting, but whatever it was, it was making'em want it way more than she'd ever seen in her years of hustlin'. She told herself she would only hold out for three more days, but then she decided to wait another full week to see the results. She had folks from out of town calling, talking about they were willing to pay anywhere from $400 to $450 just for an ounce, if she could find some. Those prices were what made her hold out a little longer. Never in her wildest dreams did she ever expect for people to be willing to pay that much for weed. Then again, why not? She was the one who was controlling the market on it anyway. Two weeks went by, and she finally decided it was time. She decided to grab fifteen more pounds, and that would leave her with thirteen more. So, she picked up the phone and called Samantha.

"Samantha, what you doing, baby?"

"Nothing, Mama. Why? Wassup?"

"I'll be down there to grab 15 of them from you or you can bring them to me early in the morning. Do you still have that scale down there?" Cha-Cha asked.

"Yeah, why? You need me to break them down for you or something?" Samantha asked.

"Naw, I'll do it."

"I'ma be leaving the house in about an hour anyway, so instead of bringing it in the morning, I can go ahead and drop'em off tonight," Samantha told her mom.

"Ok, baby. That'll be fine. Have you heard anything from your brother, lately?" Cha-Cha asked.

"Who?" Samantha said with surprise.

"Girl, you know who, so don't be playing crazy with me, because if he was going to contact anybody, it would be you. Matter of fact, you know what? Don't even answer that, because I know you have, and I know you'd lie to protect him. So, I'll just see you when you get here. Bye."

"Bye, Mama."

Samantha didn't have any idea how her mama knew so much when it came to her kids, but, somehow, she did. Samantha couldn't deny seeing Smooth, even if she wanted to. But how could her mama just outta the blue know that Samantha had seen him? One thing Samantha hoped for was that her mama's heart was softening toward her oldest child.

Cha-Cha had never asked about him before, so maybe Samantha's prayers were being answered.

Cha-Cha was now on the phone putting the word out that she would be back in business as of the next day. She had 240 ounces to sell, but regardless of how much she had to sell, she would always tell them she only had a few. She knew when she told them she only had a little, they would want to buy it all every time, but she wasn't going to sell over six ounces to any one person. She felt like if she sold too much to one client, they'd be able to control the market, and that's something she couldn't allow just yet. No matter what, at the end of this, she would have $84,000 plus her $70,000 which would give her $154,000. Knowing that she would take out $4,000 for herself to spend and a $150,000 saved up with thirteen pounds left, she was now starting to looove the drought.

For some strange reason, she had her daughter, Baby Girl, on her mind today, and she was missing her. She hadn't talked to or seen Baby Girl in almost two months now. Cha-Cha was starting to worry about Baby Girl's well-being. She was starting to think to herself that she needed to have a get together with her kids and a select few of her friends. She even thought about telling Samantha to bring Smooth, since she was the only one who knew where he was. Cha-Cha called and left word for Nathan and Charlie to come to the apartment as soon as they got the message. If they weren't there by the time she'd gotten over there, she would send Samantha to go find them and bring them back to the apartment. It had been days since she had seen either of them, but she needed a break, and now break time was clearly over. She was shocked to see Nathan and Charlie in the car with Samantha when she pulled up.

"Where in the hell did you get them two from?" Cha-Cha asked as they made their way into the apartment.

"I seen'em walking on my way over here," Samantha told her.

"You called and said for us to come over here. Now you're acting like it's a problem crazy lady," Nathan said while carrying the cooler through the door.

"Who the hell you think you talkin' to like that?" Cha-Cha said, while slapping him upside the head as he passed by on his way inside.

"Wassup, shawty? What's the problem, lil lady?" Charlie asked.

"Ain't no problem. I just ain't seen y'all in a few days, and y'all hadn't called," Cha-Cha pouted.

"Awwww, she been missing us. Ain't that tweeeet?" Nathan said jokingly.

"Shut the hell up, boy! Plus, I got something to tell y'all two. Samantha knows where Smooth at," Cha-Cha told the guys.

Samantha, who was walking past her mama, stopped dead in her tracks and turned around. She looked at her mama with a shocked look on her face. She then looked at Charlie and Nathan, who were now smiling, because they knew Cha-Cha was right.

"Mama, how you just gonna insinuate that I know where that boy is at?" Samantha said while dropping her head.

"That's how! Because every time you try to lie to me you look at the floor," Cha-Cha told her.

Nathan and Charlie just burst out laughing!

"Busted!" they both said to Samantha.

"One thing about it, lil sis?....she know all of us like a muthafucka," Nathan reminded Samantha.

"Man, don't she though, 'cause she called it right out. But I can't let you hurt my brother, Mama," Samantha told her.

"Look, enough of that shit. Nathan and Charlie, I'm gonna need y'all to help me break down these fifteen pounds to ounces. That way I'll have them ready by tomorrow, so these folks can come to pick'em up," Cha-Cha told them.

"How many of them are we going to make?" Nathan asked.

"240," Cha-Cha told him.

"240? Damn! It's going to take us the rest of the day and part of the night to finish that," Nathan told her.

"Well alrighty then, I guess we better get started Mr. Nathan," Cha-Cha replied.

An hour after they got started breaking down the weed, Cha-Cha got a call from one of her customers in South Carolina, even though she had not broadcasted to everyone just yet. though she had put the word out earlier to many. She hadn't been able to reach everyone, and this was one of the sweet ones.

"Hello?" Cha-Cha answered.

"Can I speak to Cha-Cha?" Jerome asked.

"This is me!"

"Hey, this is Jerome. Is you good? If so, me and three more of my partners wanna buy six ounces apiece. We need some bad. We can't keep it long enough, no matter how much we get," he told her.

"I know the feeling, but hit me back in a few hours. Let me see what I can come up with for you. I did just get some in, and it's already sold, but I think my people might have some."

"Alright. I'll call you back in three hours. Is that enough time, or you can call me back if you find out something before then," he told Cha-Cha.

"Will do."

"Ok, bye."

After she hung up, she told everybody what was just said.

"Do ya'll know one of my customers from, Jerome, South Carolina just called saying he wants 24 ounces and he's willing to pay $450 apiece for them. He's trying to act like it's him and three more people who want six ounces each, but I know better than to fall for that. He's trying to get more for himself because he knows I won't give more than six to one person. But for what he is willing to pay, he can have 'em."

"I know that's right, Mama. That's $10,800," Samantha said after doing some math real quick. Then she added, "One thing I do know, if you want to sell it to 'em, then I sho will."

"This shit movin like that, shawty? Why you ain't gave us none to sell yet?" Charlie asked her.

"Oh yeah, homeboy, you weren't here on the last re-up. Mama caught a damn good deal. Tyrone have her thirty pounds for 20 stacks before he went out of town, and it was his last thirty. So of course, she the only one with it, and she skinning these niggas like they catfish," Nathan told Charlie.

Charlie just looked at her, smiling, because he knew their time would soon come.

"Look, I'ma make sure all y'all get more than enough when he gets back in town and I re-up. But I had to handle this on my own because of what I'm trying to do," Cha-Cha told Charlie.

"Well, I'm just waiting shawty, 'cause I'ma fuck the 'ville up with this shit right here," Charlie told her.

"How many pounds you got left anyway?" Nathan asked Cha-Cha.

"After I move these, I'm gonna have thirteen left. Nathan, you and Charlie don't know, but I sold 10 pounds, divided up into ounces, and made $56,000 in three days. So, now I'm looking to do the same thing with these fifteen pounds right here. After I sell all twenty-four of these for $450 apiece and get these ten bands and some change, the other 216 ounces should be gone in no more than four days tops," she told them.

"And then we'll celebrate," she thought to herself.

Two hours later, she called Jerome back and told him that he could come pick up the weed tomorrow, if he still wanted it. But, it would be $450 an ounce. When he told him, she could hear the excitement in his voice. It confirmed what she already knew, that it was only him and no-one else. But she played the game right along with him, because at the end of the day, it was all business, nothing personal.

"Make sure you come by yourself, because I don't care to meet any of your partners," she told Jerome.

"OK. You should know I ain't bringing nobody else with me anyway," he reassured her.

It seemed like as soon as she got off the phone with him everybody started calling back with the same phrase, "I got three partners who wanna get six too. Can you help them?"

She told everyone the same thing, "Hit me back in a few hours, let me see what I can do."

She felt since everybody wanted to play their lil game to get more, she would play too and jack up the prices to $450. At least 5 to 10 more people called claiming to have three more partners with them now. She would only be able to serve five of them like that, and they would all be from out of town. She did the math after getting off the phone....220 out of 240 ounces was already sold, and it was going to bring in $99,000, and she would still have 20 ounces left to sell. That would bring in another $7,000, because she would sell it for $350 to people in her area.

When she really thought about it, and it actually hit her....

"Aaaaaaaaaaaaaah!!!" she just screamed, "Goddamnit, I did it!!! After tomorrow, I might just end the drought. Then again, maybe not, who knows?"

"What the hell done got into you Mama?" Samantha asked.

"Yeah, lil girl, wassup? You ain't lost it, have you?" Nathan asked.

"Shiiit, shawty, fill us in!" Charlie added.

"What the fuck is going on is that tomorrow after all this is gone, or at least most of it will be by noon or 3 pm, I will have somewhere between $99,000 and $106,000 in no fucking time. Plus, I will still have thirteen pounds of this shit left. I'm shooting to make a quarter of a million dollars or as close to it as I can get. Can y'all believe it? An ex-alcoholic from nothing to something!!" Cha-Cha explained with excitement and anticipation in her voice.

Samantha, Charlie, and Nathan just sat there dumfounded with big smiles on their faces. In a way, they couldn't believe what they were hearing, it was like it was too good to be true. But true it was, and it was coming from the only person capable of making it happen---their mama.

"What the hell!!!" Nathan exclaimed.

"I don't know why you acting surprised Nathan. I told you my plans from day one, and now that you're seeing it, you can't believe it, huh?" Cha-Cha said to him.

"Yeah, you right. I just didn't think it was gonna be like this," he told her.

"I told you: look, listen, and learn," she reminded him.

"One thing I can say about you shawty is, you don't play when it comes to getting your money," Charlie chimed in.

"Hell, I can't. I got ya'lls over-grown asses to take care of," Cha-Cha said.

"Mama, we're about to be rich!!" Samantha exclaimed..

"I gotta long way to go baby, but I'm damn sho trying to get there. I want you to go rent a car today, too. Park it on the next street in back of us, in front of Ms. Caroline's apartment. Because as soon as I get $100,000, I want it out of here ASAP. Nathan and Charlie, I want y'all here all night, so that tomorrow when she gets ready to take the money out of here, y'all will be with her. I want y'all to ride all the way to her apartment with guns in hand," she told them.

"You want me to go and get the car now? Why don't you want me to use my car?" Samantha asked Cha-Cha.

"Because everybody knows your car, and your car will be driven away by you today, and you'll return in the rental tonight out back at 2 o'clock in the morning," Cha-Cha told her.

"Yes, ma'am. I'm going now to handle this," Samantha said. As she was getting up to leave, she bid them goodnight, "see y'all in the morning."

"Ok, sis," Nathan said.

"Bye shawty," Charlie said.

"Say, you might as well go head and stay with your plan about the drought. You still got about three more weeks before Tyrone comes back in town anyway. Plus, the reason why you created the drought was so you could get all you could get anyway. So, get it while the getting is good, lil' lady. Don't let up now," Nathan told her.

"He damn sho right, shawty. Get all you can now, ain't no sense in letting up now!" Charlie added in.

With that, she made up her mind that the drought would continue, because they was right. It was the reason why she created it in the first place: so she could get all she could. The next time the drought would last two weeks, and she would only sell twelve of the thirteen pounds so she at least had one to keep for herself.

Eleven hours later, they were almost done breaking down the fifteen pounds, but before she could get finished, Droup came in from work. He just stopped and stood there looking from the doorway. He saw all the individual, aluminum foil packets lined up on the bed. He knew they were ounces, but he had never seen so many at one time, and he could understand why she hadn't cooked him dinner. She had been in their bedroom all day with her weed. He said nothing and turned to go back downstairs when she stopped him.

"Droup!" she called as he turned back around and looked at her without saying a word.

"I'm sorry, what do you want to eat? I been up here all day doing this, and the time slipped away from me. Your food should've been ready," she said to Droup.

"Go on and finish doin' what you're doin', because my food wasn't as important. Just don't let that goddamn shit make you forget again. I'm gonna go get me some Church's Chicken. I'll be back," he told her, then turned around and walked off.

"It won't make me forget again," she called after him as he walked away.

"Man, I thought he was about to go the fuck off, 'cause you know that man don't play about his food. I was ready to get the fuck outta the way," Nathan said.

"I'm talking about he didn't say one word, shawty. I'm damn near grown, and that look still scares the shit outta me," Charlie added in.

"I'll be sure to make it up to him this weekend, plus I'll explain it to him later tonight. Let's go in Punkin's room and finish these last four pounds," she told them.

"Me and Charlie can finish these; you go and make him some cheese and rice and salmon, 'cause that chicken isn't going to be enough for him. Most especially if he stops by the plaza," Nathan said.

"You damn sho right. Y'all go on, and take the rest of that to Punkin's room while I go cook him something," she told them.

"Gotcha," they said in unison.

They cleaned up and went to Punkin's room and were done three hours later. They headed downstairs with 240 ounces in the cooler and about 20 joints rolled up.

Chapter 17

The next morning everything was going as planned. Samantha had gotten the rental car, and it was parked on the back street. Charlie and Nathan were still at the apartment. Cha-Cha's phone had started ringing at 8:30 in the morning and didn't stop until around 11am. The whole time, everyone who called was making sure she was ready. Jerome was the first to come through at 9:45 am buying 24 ounces. Then right after he left, James, Pete, Ted, and Joe started pulling up 30 to 50 minutes of one another. They came from South Carolina, North Carolina, Tennessee, Rome (GA) respectively. In no time, she had $99,000, and it had come faster than she expected. She had twenty ounces left, and they were already sold in the next hour and a half. So by 12:30 pm, her mission was almost complete. They counted out a 100 Grand together, put it in a big purse and headed out the back door. Nathan had his Uzi and Charlie had a .357 Bulldog. Cha-Cha told Samantha to call her when she got home to let Cha-Cha know she had made it home safe and sound.

RING! RING! RING!

"Hello?" Cha-Cha said into the phone.

"We made it home, Mama. I'm at the apartment," Samantha told her.

"Ok, go on and put everything up, and tell Nathan and Charlie to drive the rental car back over to the apartment," Cha-Cha told her.

"What about me?" Samantha asked.

"What about you? You stay there at your apartment until it's time for you to come and take the rental car back," she told Samantha.

"Yes, ma'am. See you tonight, Mama."

"Bye, baby."

Nathan and Charlie pulled back up 20 minutes later in the rental car. They got out and walked in the apartment with smiles on their faces, because all their mama's hard work was finally paying off, and they knew she deserved it.

"Ok shawty, there anything else you need us to do?" Charlie asked.

"Yeah, light up one of those joints so that I can relax," Cha-Cha told him.

She had just about completed all her sales, and now it was time for her to get her smoke on, and to enjoy some good food with her husband and babies. Today she would surprise Droup by cooking a Roast with potatoes, onions, and carrots all chopped up. She would also cook rice, turnip greens with ham hocks, macaroni and cheese, and cornbread. She knew he loved sweet tea, so she made him a pitcher of that, too. Out of her extra $6,000, she would give him $2,000 for himself, and then send Punkin and Enos shopping with $1,000 that weekend. She also gave Charlie $1,000, since he missed out last time.

"What's this for Shawty?" Charlie asked.

"It's for you since you weren't here last time when I gave Nathan and Samantha money," she told him.

"Thanks, lil lady!" he told her.

"You ain't gotta thank me, you one of mines," and they both smiled.

But the thought of Baby Girl and Smooth was on her mind, and she told them to see what they would say.

"You all know Smooth and Baby Girl have been on my mind lately. I mean, I love'em, and at the same time, the shit that they do makes me hate'em. But with me making all this money and being at odds with them, it's kinda messing with me," she admitted to them.

Nathan and Charlie weren't the least bit surprised, because they knew she had a heart of gold, and it was just a matter of time before she let it soften towards Smooth and Baby Girl.

"I knew yesterday when you mentioned his name when we first got here. I'm going to be honest... Charlie is your cousin by blood, but you raised him as your son, therefore, you is his mama after Dora. Me, on the other hand, is a nigga you saved from the streets, and I love you for it. It's just like you're my real mama, 'cause all you've ever showed me was love and that you're my mama, and I'm your son. But, on the other hand, Baby Girl and Smooth came from you, and they're your real flesh and blood. You and Baby Girl might not ever get along, because you and her are too much alike. But she's yours. Smooth is just sick with a real bad drug problem right now that only him and God can fix. But when you think about it, before Smooth had his drug problem, he held his sisters down, and that's why Samantha and the others love him so much. See, they know he has a good heart, but it's just corrupted and being controlled by a very powerful demon right now. But when it's all said and done, they both are your children, and you know them better than any of us do. So, do whatever your heart is telling you to do," Nathan said.

"What you got to say, homeboy?" Cha-Cha asked Charlie.

"He said it all, shawty, shiiit. But he's right though," Charlie told her.

"I know he is, that's why I'm .going to bring them over here this weekend and talk to both of them," she told them.

Later that day when her husband walked through the door after he'd gotten off work, she made sure his food was ready. As soon as he walked through the door, she asked him, "You ready for your plate now or do you want it later? It's up to you," Cha-Cha said.

"What is it?" Droup asked her.

"A lil' something special to make up for yesterday. Now is you ready to eat or what?" she asked.

"Yeah, go ahead and fix me a plate while I go wash up," he told her.

"Oh yeah, grab your money out of your sock drawer too," she said.

"What money?" he asked.

"Your money, now go on and stop questioning me," she joked with him.

He just looked at her smiling before he walked off.

"Damn, Droup. You ain't going to speak to us?" Nathan asked.

"Boy, I ain't see y'all old asses sitting there, hell! But, wassup?" Droup responded.

They knew he was in a good mood when he said more than one word and they both just looked at Cha-Cha smiling, because she knew her family like the back of her hand.

"Trying to learn how to get money like you and your wife," Nathan told him.

"I know that's right, Amen"

Droup then went upstairs, laughing, to look in his sock drawer to count his money. He pulled it out and counted it, he was shocked to see $2,000 more after Cha-Cha had given him $3,000 just a few weeks ago. He thought she must be doing really well for herself now. Then he went and washed up and waited on his food. When she did bring it to him, and he saw it, the first thing he said was, "Damn, who died?"

"Ain't no damn body died. Shut up!"

"You sho know how to make up, don't you?" Droup flirted.

"I guess you can say that," she responded.

"Now the only thing I'm missing is getting a lil lovin' tonight," he said, pulling her close to him.

"You just might get what you missin' tonight lover boy." she smiled and purred playfully.

"Aww hell, now I know something's wrong. A Sunday dinner on a Thursday, $2,000, and some lovin'?! Hell, I'd be surprised if I even wake up in the morning," he said laughing out loud.

"Go to hell. You know I made over $100,000 this morning and don't know how it happened so fast.... It's already down at Samantha's apartment," Cha-Cha told him.

"Oh yeah. What you planning on doing with that money, Cha-Cha? You ain't gonna be able to keep all that money down at Samantha's forever," he told her.

"I know. We'll talk about it when I get rid of these last twelve pounds I got. I'm also thinking about having another get together this weekend for us and a few friends," she told Droup.

"Who's us?" Droup asked.

"Me, you, the kids, and a few friends."

"Ok, and that's it," he said.

"I know," she said. She then turned and left to go call Samantha.

"Hello?" Samantha answered.

"Samantha," Cha-Cha said.

"Ma'am?"

"I want you to bring Smooth over here tomorrow or you can take me to him. Either way I need to talk to him, so call him now or you can go and see him and tell him what I said," Cha-Cha told her.

"Mama, you know that boy is scared to come and see you or even call you," Samantha told her.

"Well, goddammit call him and tell him I said to call me right damn now. Let him know if I wanted him dead, then he would be dead," she told Samantha.

"Yes, ma'am, I'm about to do it right now."

Chapter 18

After Samantha got off the phone with her mama, she sat and thought about what Cha-Cha had just told her about having Smooth found and killed if she still wanted to. What her mama said was right, because Cha-Cha could've easily had someone follow Samantha and she'd have led them straight to Smooth without meaning to. Maybe Cha-Cha had already done that. Now she was confused, but either way, her mama had never lied to her. So, Samantha decided she would go ahead and go by the hotel and speak to Smooth before she took the rental car back later. Twenty some minutes later, she pulled up at the hotel, looked around before she got out of the car, and knocked on the door. When he opened up the door, she could tell he was high, she just looked at him and walked into the room. Surprised, she halted suddenly when she saw a white girl sitting on the bed, also getting high.

"Look, she needs to go. We need to talk about mama," Samantha told Smooth.

"Mama! What about her?" Smooth asked.

"She can either go stand outside or walk to the store and come back. But for now, she's gotta go, boy," Samantha said.

"Is mama out there now!?" Smooth said, in a real panic, running to the window peeking out it.

"Where she at Samantha, huh?" Smooth asked with panic in his voice.

The white girl got up saying, "Smooth, I'll be back, Ok? I'ma give y'all thirty minutes and then I'll be back."

Then the girl left.

Smooth hadn't heard a thing she said, because he had gone into "panic mode."

"Boy, calm down! Mama ain't out there, she's at home. You paranoid, now calm down." Samantha told him.

When he finally did calm down, after a few minutes, he asked, "What about mama?"

"She said to call her so she can talk to you and to get your ass over to the apartment," Samantha told him.

"Man I ain't goin over there, so she can kill me. You crazy? But I will call her though," Smooth told her.

"Boy, if Mama wanted to find you, she could easily find you. Hell, she already knows that I know where you at."

"How!? You musta told her? You told mama where I'm at, Samantha?"

"Naw, I ain't told her nothin'! You must have forgotten that Mama knows all of us better than we know ourselves? Have you forgotten that, Smooth? How many times has Mama known something and nobody had to tell her? Huh?"

His high had started to come down, and reality had start to set in, and he knew his sister was right. Didn't nobody have to tell his mama nothing when it came to them. She always knew. How? Nobody knew!!

"Ok, I'ma call her," Smooth told her.

"Do it before you start getting high again, boy. I'm on my way back over there now, because I gotta take her rental car back before the place closes."

"Rental car? Mama can't drive," Smooth said, confused.

"She rented it for something she had to do. Now the same way she rented that one, she could've easily rented another one and had me followed to find you, if she wanted to. Now you see why I say you're safe?

"Yea. I'm about to call her now. Hold on, don't you go nowhere so you can see what she gotta say to me."

He then picked up the phone in his room and dialed his mama's number. She answered on the third ring.

"Hello?"

"Hey Mama," He said into the phone with tremble in his voice.

"SMOOTH!!!?"

"Yep this-." Before he even answered she cut him off.

"Before you say anything else! You need to praise the goddamn ground that that girl walks on. She's the only reason why I haven't killed your ass. She cried like a goddamn baby for you 'cause I was going to bury your ass, boy."

"I know. I'm sorry, Mama."

"No, the hell you ain't. How many times you done told that same damn lie about you being sorry? But look, brang your ass over here tonight or tomorrow. I ain't go'n fuck witchu. Only because of her, she can brang you herself, and don't be acting like you so scared, because if you was so fucking scared you wouldn't have stolen my goddamn money. I ain't playing with your ass either---you better be over here. Now put your sister on the phone, 'cause I know she's standing there."

He just handed her the phone without saying another word.

"Ma'am?" Samantha said.

"Have his ass over here tonight or tomorrow. And what time is you taking that car back?"

"I'm on my way now, and he'll be there tomorrow."

"He better be. Bye." And Cha-Cha hung up

Chapter 19

The next day Cha-Cha had called Baby Girl, and Sheila told them to come over to the apartment. Baby Girl was surprised that her mama even called her and to tell her to come over. She thought that either she was dreaming or in a make-believe conversation with her mama. Cha-Cha had already made plans for Samantha and Smooth to come over the day before, so now she just had to call Droup at work.

"Yea." Droup said as he got on the phone.

"Don't you get off work early today since, it's Friday?" Cha-Cha asked him.

"Yea. I should be off at two o'clock. Why?"

"Cause I want you to stop by the liquor store and the grocery store, and pick up the stuff for this weekend," Cha-Cha told him.

"Wright it down, and have it ready for me when I get home. I'll go back out and pick it up after I get cleaned up. I don't see why you just don't have Samantha take you to the store and you pick it up."

"Cause I want you to do it. Plus, Samantha's goin to be here wit me, Sheila, Baby Girl and Smooth."

"Wit who!?" He said. He couldn't believe the other two names of his kids he was hearing.

"You heard me the first time. So don't be acting like you didn't hear what I said."

"Hell, I'm trying to make sure. You must got a fever or something or you comin' down with the flu. You ain't goin crazy on me is you?" Droup asked her.

"Go to hell! I'll see you when you get home. Bye," Cha-Cha told him.

"Yea a'ight. Bye."

Cha-Cha sat thinking about the next two weeks and the last twelve pounds she had to get rid of. She had to keep one for herself, but she would probably still sell some of it. One thing she knew was that she had to have her personal stash at all times. She had held out for two weeks only once, and that was when Tyrone first went out of town. Now since he was on his way back in the next three weeks, she would use two of them as the remaining of the drought she had created. She knew her prices would drop back down, now that he was on his way back. One thing else she knew; the more you buy, the less you pay. She had a good idea to spend no less than $50,000 but no more than $75,000 when he did get back in town. Or, she might just take the money she made off the twelve pounds and spend it all with him. She just hadn't decided yet.

The downstairs door opened and closed, and she heard all four of her oldest kids coming up the steps.

"Mama, you up here!?" Samantha called out.

"Yea, I'm up here!"

She knew Smooth was going to be the last one in line, because he didn't know what to expect, and he was going to need running room just in case he did have to run. When all of'em got into the room, Cha-Cha just sat there and stared at Smooth for a few seconds, but it seemed like forever before she spoke. The rest of'em just stood there not saying anything, because nobody wanted to interrupt her and make her mad.

"Look at me! Dammit! Don't be looking at the fuckin floor!" Cha-Cha said to him.

He raised his head and looked at the woman who gave birth to him. As soon as he did, she got off the bed and slapped the shit out of'm.

"Mama! Don't be hittin him like that." Samantha said while Sheila and Baby Girl just looked.

"Shut the hell up! I promised you I wouldn't kill 'em or hurt 'em, but I ain't say shit about not slapping the shit out of'm!"

"Boy, you musta really fucked up for her to slap the shit outta you like that." Baby Girl said.

"Oh, so you don't know? Mr. Smooth, here, stole $1,575.00 from me about a month ago and been hiding ever since. The only reason why I had a change of heart from burying his ass is because of Samantha. She's been defending him and crying for his goddamn ass from day one. And not to mention, she's been hiding him and feeding him with my money. Yea, I can tell...just look at him and smell him...He looks like Samantha and my money been takin' care of his thievin' ass...smell better, new clothes...new haircut...a hell of a lot better lookin than when he stole my damn money. From Ho-bo to So-So wit a long ass way to go," teased Cha-Cha.

Baby Girl covered her mouth to keep from laughing, then looked at Smooth. "Boy is you crazy to steal from your mama? I might be stupid, but I ain't crazy or gotta fuckin' death wish. You really need help, boy."

"Slap his ass again, Mama! He need it." Sheila said, slapping Smooth upside the head. "Boy, will you ever learn? Damn!"

His mama was about to slap him again, but let it go.

"So, you goin to stand up there looking fuckin stupid and holding your face? You ain't got a goddamn thing to say, besides sorry? Because that, I don't wanna hear it…I've been hearing lies since you was a child, so I know you don't mean that."

"What else is there to say, Mama? I fucked up. I'm a junkie. I mean, we all know I need help, but if I'm not ready to get help… What good would goin to rehab do?" Smooth asked.

She just stood there listening, stunned, because out of everything he'd ever said out of his mouth, she felt this was the truth, and she told'm.

"You know that might be the truest shit you ever spit out of that lying ass mouth of yours."

"If I stood here and tried to lie, you'd know. So, I might as well tell the truth."

"'Bout damn time. But if you ever steal from me again, so help me God. I'ma kill your black ass--- dead as a door knob. You hear me, boy?"

"Yes, ma'am I hear you."

"Now the reason why I wanted y'all over here is because I'm having a get together for all my kids and a few of my friends. Of all my kids, y'all two are the only ones I ever have problems outta." She said pointing to Smooth and Baby Girl.

"Baby Girl, I can't stand you, but everyone is right. You're just like me, a spitting fuckin image. I do love you and want us to start tryin to get along, even if it is for a short time."

"Mr. Smooth, no matter what I do or say, you always rebel against me, and I'm sick of it. You are my oldest child, and I do remember when you used to be one of the sharpest and smartest men I knew. What happened to you, I don't know, but I do wish I could get him back. Either way, you're still my child, and I don't wanna turn my back on you again. But so help me God, I will if I have to. Here me good now...so please, don't make me do it.

"Sheila and Samantha, I ain't never really had to worry about y'all. So, can we all just try to get along at least for the weekend, then we can go from there, huh?" Cha-Cha asked from the heart.

Everyone in the room knew she was talking to Smooth and Baby Girl, and they both agreed with their mama.

"Y'all know I miss the hell outta both of y'all, right?" Cha-Cha asked them.

"I miss you too mama." Smooth said hugging her neck.

"Hmm...sho do smell better," A pleased Cha-Cha quasi-whispered.

"I can't stand you either, Mama. But I love you to death and I miss you too," Baby Girl said, also hugging her mama's neck.

"Ok y'all that's enough....y'all goin to make me cry." Samantha said with tears in her eyes.

Then they all sat around laughing, talkin and joking till they heard a truck pull up on the side of the apartment. Baby Girl knew by instinct that it was their daddy. She went to the side bathroom window and looked out as soon as she saw it was him.

The first thing she said was, "There goes my daddy!!"

She took off running out the room downstairs and clean out the front door straight to her daddy giving him a hug.

"Hey daddy!!! I missed you," she told him.

"Hey gurrrl. Wat you doin over here, I thought you and your ma was mad at each other?"

"Naw, she called all us over here, and she talked to us. She said she's tired of fighting wit us."

"Oh yea?"

"Yea, I don't know how long it's goin to last though. You know how your wife is. She's crazy, daddy."

"Hell, where you think you get it from?" Droup asked her.

"I know right," Baby Girl replied.

And they both started laughing.

"Smooth is over here too."

"He be lucky if I don't hit him in his goddamn mouth for stealing from her."

"I just found out not too long ago. And you know, she already done slapped the shit out him."

"He better be glad she didn't shoot his ass."

"I know. He was scared as hell too, Daddy."

They continued to talk 'til they got upstairs to the bedroom door. Soon as they hit the door, Samantha pushed Baby Girl outta the way.

"Move, girl let me hug my daddy. Hey Daddy."

"Hey fat gurl."

"How was your day?"

"Uhh, it was Ok"

"Hey, Daddy." Sheila said also hugging him.

Smooth just looked at him, because he didn't know what to expect.

"What's your goddamn problem boy? Huh? Stealing from your mama. You want me to hit you in your goddamn mouth?"

"Naw, Daddy."

"Do it again, and I'ma come and find you my goddamn self and do some hell to ya. Yo' ma work too damn hard for her money for you to come and steal it from her. You hear me?"

"Yes sir."

"You better! 'Cause I ain't playing witcha. She gotta love you to have your ass back in here. You better be glad she ain't shot the shit outta your ass," Droup told him.

"I know, that woud be kinda messy " Smooth replied.

The whole time Droup was talking, no one dared to say anything, complete silence. Everyone just looked at Smooth with a 'Hmn, you in trouble again' look on their faces.

"Where's that list that I told you to make out while I was at work, so I can go get this food and stuff you want?" Droup asked Cha-Cha.

"I been in here wit them since we got off the phone. It slipped my mind."

She then reached in her pouch and counted out a thousand dollars and gave it to'm.

"Huh, just go get some Ribs, chicken, Rib eyes steaks, Hamburger meat, and some hot dogs. Get some beer, liquor, chips, buns, charcoal fluid, cups, paper plates, soda and whatever you know we might need. That should be enough money to cover all of that.

When you stop by the plaza, tell Hot Pocket them to come over tomorrow 'cause I'm havin another get together. Tell'm don't bring no-damn-body else with them either, and if you have some change left, buy 'em something to eat and something to drink for the day," Cha-Cha told him.

When he got ready to turn and walk out the door, Baby Girl said, "I'm goin' witchu Daddy."

Everyone just looked at her, 'cause every time she was around their daddy she turned into a big ass baby. Well, she was the baby of the girls.

"How you know I want you to go wit me?" He said jokingly.

"'Cause I'm your baby and you love me. That's how I know."

"That don't mean I want you to go though," he said jokingly.

"Yes, it do. Now come on, let's go so we can hurry up and get back." She said, as she grabbed his arms and pulled him out the door all the way down to the car.

Cha-Cha got on the phone and called JJ and Harold. Then she told Sheila to call DeWayne, and tell'm about tomorrow. Right then Smooth's mind went to wondering, *"Could this be a setup to actually kill me?"*

"Momma what about me?" Smooth asked.

"What about you, boy?"

"You calling the same ones who tried to kill me," he reminded her.

"Annnd. So what? They ain't go'n fuck witchu unless I say so," she told him.

"You should already know that, boy. You still high?" Sheila said.

"Naw, ain't nobody high, girl."

"Well stop acting paranoid, then," Sheila told him.

"Long as I'm around, ain't nobody gonna touch my big brother any way. Ain't that right, Mama?" Samantha said.

"If you say so Ms. Samantha. But I damn sho would like to know who died and left you in charge. Because my baby is gonna run this."

"What baby, Enos!?" Smooth said.

"Nope...Punkin. She's already preparing him now at 10 years old to take over if nothing goes wrong." Sheila said.

"What the hell?! Mama, you mean to tell me, you got my 10-year-old lil brother being groomed to be a drug dealer."

"First off, you ain't got no fuckin business questioning me about what I'm doing. Secondly, I can't be fucking trusting you. Look at what you're doing. And I can't trust Baby Girl either. Samantha is doing something else when it comes to me, and Sheila just don't have the damn nerves. Look, we're just goin to leave this alone. Ok"

"Na--." Before he got it out of his mouth, he was cut off.

"Smooth! Leave it alone boy. Trust me. Me, Baby Girl and Daddy have already been cursed out 'bout this, so just quit while you're ahead." Sheila said.

Smooth just stood there shaking his head.

Chapter 20

Punkin had finally gotten the chance to hit the block with his big brother Nathan, to see what was going on in the streets for real. He already had a little experience from just being home watching his mama and going out with his brother, Charlie, from time to time. For some reason though, he knew this would be way different than anything he had ever witnessed.

"You know why I haven't brought you out with me, right?" Nathan asked Punkin.

"Naw. Why not?" Punkin asked.

"Because mama been had us looking for Smooth. You know he stole over $1,500 from mama not too long ago."

"Hell naw, I ain't know--- that's why I hate that bitch ass nigga. He ain't no brotha of mines, period."

"Watch your mouth boy, he's still your big brotha."

"No, he ain't! You and Charlie is my big brothas. He can't tell me nothing, period, for real. And if he tried, I'd swang on'm."

"And he'd beat your lil ass too. You better not let Mama know I told you about that either. A'ight."

"You know I ain't go'n say nothin," Punkin told him.

They were now walking up Gorland street to get to Shaw street so they could cut across the rent office lawn to get to Pryor Road. Nathan pulled out a joint, fired it up and passed it to Punkin. He always let him smoke, 'cause their mama let'm smoke. But this was the first time he got the chance to smoke outside in the open.

"This that new weed mama got y'all, call Tie Stick?" Punkin said inhaling the smoke.

"Hell naw boy! You couldn't handle that weed, hell, it's too strong for us. What you trying to do nigga, smoke up the whole damn joint? Pass my shit." An agitated Nathan said.

Punkin started laughing at his big brotha, "I didn't hit it but three times."

"Nigga, it's puff puff pass, not puff puff puff." Nathan said as they were now crossing the street on Pryor road to get to the plaza.

They came up to the Chinese store first, and Nathan saw a nigga that owed him some money. He looked at Punkin and told him, "Lesson one, when a nigga owes you money, make'm pay."

Punkin made sure he listened to every word he said.

"Now pay attention. Come on." They then walked up on some dude, and Nathan said, "Say bruh, where the fuck my money at nigga? You done had over two fuckin' weeks to pay me my shit," He said while pointing his finger in the dude's face.

"Nathan, you know I'ma pay you your money, my nigga. I just ain't had it."

Soon as he said that, Nathan punched him in the mouth, and in the face bout six or seven times. Then he pulled out his pistol and put it in the dude's face.

"Bitch-ass nigga, you better have my money today or I'ma shoot the shit outta of yo' punk ass."

"Ok man just don't shoot me. I swear I'm tryin Nathan."

"Just have my shit nigga! I don't care if you have to suck and fuck for it. But you better get it."

"Oh oh oh Ok"

Then some female said, "Nathan, leave that damn man alone, you know he's gonna pay yo' crazy ass. Damn!"

He then looked her way and raised his pistol in her direction.

"Bitch, shut the fuck up before I shoot you in your big fuckin mouth. You must wanna pay it for'm? Say bitch, answer me!" The female didn't say anything else.

"Nathan, why the fuck you fucking wit foolish Elaine? You know she ain't got good goddamn sense, man. Look my nigga, don't pay her no attention," Clyde said.

"Well, you better get that bitch then before she's at Grady with a bullet in her fuckin mouth."

"I got her. Come here girl, let's go!"

"Now pussy nigga, go get my damn money!" He forcefully said as the dude was sitting on the ground bleeding, looking up at him shaking his head.

They headed into Shawty's Barber Shop to get a haircut. Shawty was one of the best and fastest barbers on that side of town, hands down.

"Wassup Shawty? Me and Punkin need a haircut." Nathan said.

"A'ight I gotcha. Wassup lil man? How's your mama doing?" Shawty said.

"Wassup Shawty. She good," Punkin told him.

"Nathan is you ever going to stop being so goddamn hot headed?"

"Shiiiit shawty, these pussy niggas better pay me or pay the piper."

Shawty just looked at Nathan with a smile on his face. Thirty minutes later, they both had their fresh cuts and headed across the street to the plaza. But while they were on the way, Nathan started explaining everything to Punkin.

"You can't be no pussy or soft hearted when it comes to these hoe ass niggas or these punk ass bitches, 'cause they will take your kindness for weakness fast as hell. You hear me nigga?"

"Yea, I hear you big bruh. Was you really gonna shoot that girl?"

"Wat you think? Hell yea, I was gonna shoot that bitch. She better learn how to keep her muthafuckin mouth closed," he said as they were crossing the street called Joyland Place to get to the plaza.

As they were approaching the plaza, Punkin noticed all the dudes from the last time when his mama, daddy, lil brother, and he were up there getting something to eat. Punkin also noticed his cousin, Denver, and his crew. You could hear Denver's mouth all the way across the parking lot over everyone else out there. No matter what he was talking about or who he was talking to you, you were gonna hear him.

"Wassup Nathan? What the hell you doing wit this lil bad ass nigga here wit you?" Denver said showing a mouth full of golds.

"Shit. I got him out here getting ready for the streets. Cha-Cha's orders."

"Ooohh shit! Ain't the lil nigga bad enough as it is?"

"Hey. What she says, we do." Nathan said, shrugging his shoulders and throwing his hands up in surrender.

"Yea I know. Wassup lil bad ass nigga, you got some weed for sale? I see you out here with your big brotha, so I don't doubt it," Denver said to Punkin.

"Wassup cuz? Naw, they won't give me none yet. Said I gotta wait a while," Punkin explained.

"Let me catch you selling some weed… I'ma beat your ass," Denver threatened.

"Nigga, you ain't gonna put your hands on me. My mama will beat your ass if you hit me."

"Dats your muthafuckin problem now, nigga. Cha-Cha won't let nobody beat your ass. But like I said, let me catch you… I'ma be the one to beat your ass."

"Nigga, you don't want none of my mama! So, stop frontin'," Punkin told him.

"Get your lil bad ass on," Denver, their cousin, told him.

As they were walking off, Punkin heard one of Denver's workers say,

"That lil nigga is bad as hell, for real! You know he's gonna be hell just like the rest of y'all."

"Yeah, I know right? You know that's Cha-Cha's son, so he already feels like can't nobody touch him. Just look at'm, lil bad-ass...grown as hell." Punkin heard them saying as they walked away.

"Sheika! Brang your ass here girl!" Nathan called out to a thick, brown skinned girl, who was wearing some black tights, a halter top, and some black and white Nikes.

When she was walking over towards them, they could see that she was so soft that her thighs and hips just jiggled. Sheika walked straight up to Nathan, grabbed his dick, and said, "Wassup baby."

"Look, this my lil brother, Punkin, right here. Say wassup, nigga."

"Wassup shawty? You fine as a muthafucka." Punkin said grabbing his lil dick.

"Hey, baby bro. Wassup, you cute," Sheika said, looking Punkin over.

"I can be whatever you want," Punkin told her.

"Hmmm, really? I think you better wait a few more years, baby."

"Naw, I don't need to wait. I'm ready." Punkin said.

Sheika just turned to Nathan, who was standing there watching his lil brother, with a smile on his face.

"I see you trained him well, daddy," she told Nathan.

"Yeah, he in process, but he still got a few miles to go through. But what the hell you doing up here?" Nathan asked.

"Nothing, just passing thru."

"Ok, well pass your ass on thru back to the apartment. Here, get this money and this weed, and get your ass on before I get mad."

"Ok daddy, I'm gone, 'cause I sho don't want you mad at me. Thank you too, daddy."

After he gave her the money and the weed, she gave him a kiss and turned around and left. When she was walking off, her ass just jiggled like it had a mind of its own, and Nathan just watched Punkin looking at her. After she was out of sight, they walked to the cafe where they ordered something to eat. While they waited on their food, Nathan gave Punkin five dollars and told him to go get some quarters so they could play video games. Punkin went, came back, and gave him the quarters. Nathan split the coins equally between them. He kept ten quarters and gave Punkin ten. Punkin went and started playing the racecar game while Nathan played Pac-Man. Punkin saw roughly twenty people come in the café and buy weed from Nathan. The lady behind the counter called his name when their order was ready.

He went to the counter, reached in his pocket, and gave her some weed and money. Nathan served everybody. Now that business was out of the way, they sat down and ate their food. When they were done, they headed back outside and went in the back of the plaza. When they got back there, Nathan reached in his pocket, grabbed a bag of weed and some rollin' papers. He put some weed in the paper, rolled it up, and passed it to Punkin with a lighter. Punkin fixed it up, hit it twice and passed it back. They stayed back there until they finished smoking the joint. When they finished, they walked back to the front where they chilled for a couple of hours before they left and headed back to the apartment.

Chapter 21

As they were walking up the street to the apartment, Punkin noticed Samantha's car out in front and his daddy's work truck on the side street, where he always parked. Once they got closer, Punkin saw that their family's car was gone, and that only could mean one thing… Punkin's daddy wasn't home, because no one else ever drove their car except for Droup.

When they entered the apartment, Punkin heard his mama and someone, whom sounded like Smooth, talking as he led Nathan up the stairs. For reasons he hinted at with Nathan earlier, Punkin got extremely upset when he heard Smooth's voice as he got to his mama's bedroom door. He saw both his big sisters, Sheila and Samantha, then he saw his mama and Smooth.

"Mama, what he doing over here?" Punkin asked, looking at Smooth.

But before his mama had a chance to say something, Smooth spoke.

"Nigga, you don't be questioning her!" Smooth told Punkin.

"Nigga, fuck you! I'm a kill you when I get grown! I hate you! You ain't my fuckin brotha anyway!" Punkin yelled at Smooth.

Before Smooth could respond, Samantha spoke up, "Boy, you better watch your damn mouth before I spank your butt. And he is your big brotha. See, Mama," she said, looking at Cha-Cha, "that boy is getting way out of hand talking to Smooth like that."

"Punkin, what the hell is wrong with you, boy?" Sheila said, staring at Punkin waiting for him to answer.

"I hate him! I wish he would die! He don't wanna do nothin' but steal from our mama and get high. Plus, he always disrespecting Mama!" Punkin explained with hatred in his eyes.

"Mama, if you don't get that boy, I'm a beat his lil ass. Now, I ain't gonna keep standin' up here letting him disrespect me like he's grown." Smooth said.

"Punkin, enough! I told your sister to bring him over here, because I wanted to talk to him. No matter what he may or may not have done, he's still my child and your brotha. So, whether you like it or not, he's here." Cha-Cha said.

Punkin turned his head slowly panning from his mama to Smooth and replied, "My brothas names is Enos, Nathan

191

and Charlie! And nigga, don't you say nothing else to me, never in life and not even in death!"

As soon as Punkin said that, Nathan snatched him up by his shirt.

"Nigga what I done told you about your mouth when it comes to Mama, huh? Apologize to her right now or I'ma beat your ass."

"I'm sorry, Mama."

"Say it like you mean it, nigga! And hug her neck," Nathan commanded him.

"I'm sorry, Mama. I ain't gone do it no more." Punkin said while hugging his mama's neck and kissing her on the jaw.

When he got done, Nathan said, "Now, apologize to Smooth too."

"Nope! I ain't apologizing to him."

Nathan punched Punkin in the chest so hard that it knocked him down on the floor.

"I said apologize now, nigga."

"You just gonna have to beat me, 'cause I ain't doing it."

Nathan went over to him and snatched him up off the ground by his shirt and put his face in Punkin's face. Punkin didn't blink or turn his head. He looked Nathan straight in the eyes with so much hatred that Nathan just put him down and told'm, "Go to your goddamn room, nigga. I'll be in there in a minute."

Punkin went to his room, slammed the door, and sat on his bed.

"I don't care what Nathan says or do to me. I'm not apologizing to that pussy-ass nigga." Punkin thought to himself.

"Y'all better do something with that damn boy, Mama. He's too fucking grown to be 10 years old." Smooth said to Cha-Cha.

"Naw, you and Baby Girl shouldna been disrespecting me in front of him. Then, maybe he wouldn't be the way he is towards y'all. Samantha and Sheila damn sho don't be having problems out of'm like that," Cha-Cha pointed out.

"But, if I went in there and beat his lil ass, then you'd have to say something or do something to try to hurt me. And that's wrong," Smooth told her.

"Don't tell me what's wrong. What's wrong is how you mistreat us for them damn drugs, Smooth. Punkin knows what you do, and he's heard you disrespect me a bunch of times, too damn many," Cha-Cha reminded him.

"But Mama, that still doesn't give Punkin the right to disrespect Smooth." Samantha mediated.

"How can y'all expect for Punkin to respect Smooth, when Smooth don't respect me...or himself for that matter, and I'm the one who brought his disrespectful ass into this world, huh?"

"Y'all, let's just leave this thing alone, because we ain't going to get nowhere wit it. Mama, you and Smooth is trying to build y'all relationship and trust back up. And since Nathan is responsible for Punkin now, we'll let him deal wit that problem. You better deal wit it too, nigga." Sheila said, looking at Nathan with an 'I ain't playing witchu' look in her eyes.

Nathan turned around and left to go deal with Punkin. All of'em knew he wasn't goin to whip'm. He was just goin to talk to'm and maybe ruff him up some. They sat there and talked for a while longer and continued to plan the barbecue for the next day.

When Nathan returned to the room, he just stood there and panned from Smooth to Sheila to Samantha to their mama, shaking his head.

"Don't be standing there looking stupid. Did you handle him like I said or do I gotta go do it?" Samantha asked him.

"Sis, I don't see nobody in this room right now that can change his mind. He really does hate Smooth. Do you know he just asked me for my pistol to come in here and shoot him in the face? Smooth, just stay away from him, and let him calm down. Don't make his hate for you any worse than it is. If you show him something, show him you are trying to change toward this family."

"Man, y'all act like this is a grown ass man we talking about. He's a goddamn child who needs a good ass beating," Smooth said.

"Yeah, just like when your granddaddy used to tie you to the chair and beat the shit outta you. But look at you. It didn't do you no damn good, now did it." Cha-Cha said.

Smooth couldn't say nothing in response, because he knew what she said was the god honest truth, and Sheila and Samantha just looked on. Nathan stood there smiling, because just like their mama, he knew his lil brother. One thing he knew, if Punkin didn't grow outta his hate for Smooth, then Smooth had better watch his ass when Punkin got a few more years on him.

The next day they were getting ready for the get together. It would start early for the kids and carry on into the night for the adults. So, by five o'clock Harold had fixed the grill up for the hamburgers, hotdogs and chicken for the kids. He decided to grill a slab of ribs too. By 8:30 or 9pm that night all the kids were upstairs playing and watching TV, but all the grown folks were downstairs drinking, smoking, dancing, playing cards and just generally having a good time.

Punkin felt like he wasn't supposed to be upstairs with the other kids; he felt like he was supposed to be downstairs. So, he got up and went downstairs. When he entered the living room, he saw all three of his sisters and some of the dudes from the plaza on Pryor Road sitting around smoking weed and drinking liquor and beer, except Sheila, as she never smokes weed. Nobody even noticed Punkin as he walked past. He headed out the back door to where Harold was barbecuing.

"Boy, what you doing out here this time of night? You supposed to be upstairs with the rest of the kids," Harold pointed out.

"I don't wanna be up there around them. I wanna be down here with y'all," Punkin explained.

"You been hanging 'round grown folks so long, now you feel like you and other kids don't have nothin' in common," Harold pointed out.

"That's 'cause we ain't got nothin' in common," Punkin told him.

"A'ight now, I'ma let you stay out here with me, but if your ass gets in trouble because your mama or daddy comes out here and sees you, that's on you. A'ight?" Harold said.

"A'ight!" Punkin agreed.

Harold turned back around to finish cooking the meat. Punkin noticed Harold had his own cooler of beer out on the back porch, and Harold had his gun laying on the grill's wooden slats in front of the grill. Harold also had his own bag of reefer to himself. Punkin didn't see his big brother Nathan standing in the door watching him 'til, all of a sudden, the screen door opened up and Nathan walked out.

"What the hell you doing out here?" Nathan asked Punkin.

"I don't wanna be up there with them," Punkin explained.

Harold spoke up, "It's our fault Nathan, he's been hanging around us so long, now he don't feel right being around other kids. He's too advanced for'em."

"He better not let Cha-Cha or Droup catch'm here," Nathan warned.

Punkin looked through the back porch window into the kitchen where he was able to see his mama and his daddy at the table playing spades with his play-uncle, Crabby, and his play-aunt, Effie. He looked and saw Smooth and became mad instantly. Nathan saw the look in Punkin's eyes when he saw Smooth. He tapped Harold on the shoulder and pointed directing his focus to witness the hatred in Punkin's eyes toward Smooth.

"Boy, who you looking at like that?" Harold asked Punkin.

"Smooth! I hate that bitch-nigga. Let me see your gun, I'ma go shoot'm."

"Boy, that's your brotha," Harold said, trying to reason with Punkin.

"No he ain't. Enos, Nathan and Charlie is my brothas. I bet I kill'm when I get grown."

Nathan tried to explain it to Harold, "Man, he really hates Smooth, I done tried to talk some sense into him. I don't think nobody can change his mind when it comes to Smooth. I beat Punkin up yesterday trying to make'm apologize to Smooth. I mean, I hit him in the chest so hard, I knocked him on his ass, then I snatched him up. Do you know when I had him in my face and I looked in his eyes, I saw pure damn hatred for Smooth. I just made him go to his room. Then when I went to his room and threatened to beat him up and did in a way, he still bucked against me. Punkin ain't never bucked on me, bruh."

"Damn. Well, I feel him, because how can you receive from that lil lady in there and then turn around and disrespect her, stealing from her. She took all of us off the streets and loved us like no other," Harold reminded Nathan.

They then heard some loud breathing. When they turned and looked, they saw Punkin standing there breathing hard with tears running down his face. They both just looked at one another and shook their heads. Then Harold had an idea.

"Nathan, go tell Cha-Cha to stop that card game, and come eat out here. Tell her to brang Smooth with her too." He whispered to Nathan low enough so Punkin couldn't hear him.

A few seconds later Punkin saw Nathan whispering in his mama's ear, and she got up from the table, then Smooth disappeared from his eyesight. The next thing he knew, they were on the back porch.

"Look at'm y'all." Harold said.

"Boy, wat's wrong with you?" Cha-Cha asked.

"Smooth is what's wrong wit'm. Punkin came downstairs and was chilling out here wit us, then the next thang we know, he's standing in the window lookin at Smooth breathing hard and crying. I've never seen this much hate in Punkin before, and I can truly say he really hates you, Smooth." Harold said.

"Come here, baby," Cha-Cha said, reaching her arms out to hug Punkin.

Punkin walked to his mama and hugged her while she hugged him back. Smooth finally realized just how much his little brotha really hated him, but it didn't faze him at all. He was just like 'oh well' to himself and turned around getting ready to walk off, when Harold grabbed his arm.

"Look, you might not care how he feels about you right now, but with the anger and the hate he has built up inside of him for you--- it should scare you....tonight! You can go ahead and walk away and not pay it any attention like it's nothing. But in a few more years, he's gonna be skilled, street smart, taller, equipped, and a whole lot angrier than he is now. He's already wanting to shoot you in the face right fucking now! So, my advice to you....my advice to you big brotha.... is to try to get through to him 'right fucking now'....you see how that works, bruh? Before it's too late, if it ain't already," Harold strongly advised Smooth, trying to warn him of eminent danger.

Smooth just looked at Harold with a blank stare, then walked away.

"Next time he gets outta line, just let Punkin loose, and I bet you Smooth'll be dead before you could blink," Harold told Cha-Cha.

"My baby ain't nothing but 10 years old! I'm not about to let'm kill no goddamn body. Have y'all lost y'all damn minds?" Cha-Cha asked, looking at Harold then Nathan disappointingly with disapproval written all over her face.

"Naw, but that nigga Smooth has, if he thinks that Punkin will just forget or let it go. You know how Punkin holds a grudge. Hell, I'm surprised you let Smooth back around you after you had us to try to kill'm," Harold told her.

"Look, we can talk about this later. Right now, I'm tryin to enjoy myself and y'all should be tryin to do the same damn thang, but I'm telling you, I'll be damned if my baby is finna kill nobody!" Cha-Cha told them.

"Well, me, Punkin, and Nathan are about to finish sittin' out here and smoke us a joint. Don't worry. I won't let him drink, but he do needs to get high right now," Harold told her.

Cha-Cha just looked at the three of them and went back to the table and finished playing cards. So, they just stayed on the back porch and smoked about three joints back to back. Punkin got so high, he damn near passed out.

"Damn, Harold, what you do to the reefer?" Nathan asked.

"I didn't do nothing to it. I just knew his lil ass couldn't handle three of'em back to back, and I knew he'd try to hang.

So, I put it on his lil ass and knocked him out. Now you can go ahead and take 'em on back upstairs and put him in the bed," Harold said, laughing to himself.

Nathan picked Punkin up and took him in the apartment. On his way upstairs, in the living room, all eyes were on Nathan carrying Punkin without a word until Samantha spoke.

"Where he come from? I thought he was upstairs with the rest of the kids," A confused Samantha commented.

"Just goes to show how much y'all be paying attention, because he's been down here on the back porch with us for hours. He walked past all y'all, and I was the only one who spotted him," Nathan said loudly over the music and looked around at the rest of the living room crowd shaking his head side to side like a pendulum.

Nathan continued upstairs to put Punkin in bed. Just as he got to Punkin's bedroom door, he heard some sniffling coming from Sheila's room. He went and dropped Punkin off in bed and went to Sheila's door.

Knock! Knock! Knock!

"Who is it?" Sheila said.

"Nathan, girl. You Ok?" Nathan asked.

Sheila opened up the door, crying.

"Man, what the hell you crying for? Never mind, let me guess, you and DeWayne been up here arguing," Nathan guessed.

"That son of a bitch gets on my goddamn nerves. I know he fucking wit another bitch, but he thinks that I'm stupid. The mothafucka can't even spend the night wit me. He started this shit just so he could leave," Sheila told him.

"You know, I really hate getting in y'all business, because no matter what I say, you're gonna do what you wanna do anyway. So, my advice to you is to follow your heart. Now clean yourself up, come on back downstairs, and finish enjoying yourself! Girl, you gotta always remember--- he's not the only nigga on this earth."

"You right, bruh. Give me a minute--- I be down there," Sheila told him.

"You better. You too goddamn fine to be crying over any nigga," Nathan reminded her.

Sheila started smiling, because she knew he was telling her nothing but the truth. She wiped her face, calmed down, and went back downstairs to continue enjoying herself. By the time she got back down there, people had started leaving, and only a few of'em were left. The get together went on 'til about three o'clock in the morning, then they all went to sleep.

Nathan slept downstairs on the sofa, since everyone else was in their room.

Chapter 22

Enos was the first one up in the apartment the next morning. He got out of his bed and walked in Punkin's room first and saw that he was still sleeping. So, he went to his parents' room and saw both of them still sleeping also. He decided to go downstairs and see if anybody was up. He saw Nathan asleep on the couch, snoring with his mouth wide open and an empty beer bottle on the floor by the couch. Enos stood in the living room for a few seconds before he went into the kitchen and opened the refrigerator to get something to eat.

There was cake in the fridge on a plate that he just had to have. So he reached in, grabbed a piece, leaving finger marks in the rest of the cake, stuffed it in his mouth with both hands, and then wiped his hands on his shirt. He then tried to pour himself a glass of lemonade, but spilled it all over the floor. Enos looked around with a frightened look on his face, expecting someone to catch him. He knew he had messed up by spilling the lemonade but didn't realize that the cake on his shirt was a dead giveaway.

Nathan had sneaked into the kitchen and watched Enos just to see what he was going to do next, before he disturbed him. He watched Enos as he went and grabbed the mop and tried to clean up his mess. Nathan just stood continuing to watch his baby brother, then he scared him. He jumped out into te open making a big noise with his fleet.

"Boy, what you doin!?" Nathan belted out.

Enos jumped, and at the same time, dropped the mop. He turned around, looking scared, 'cause he knew he was busted.

"Umm noffin." Enos said, trying to pivot from a scared look to innocent.

"So, you just go'n sit here in my face and tell me a lie and you got lemonade all over the floor and cake all on your shirt? Go on to the table and sit down while I clean up this mess and clean you up before Mama wake up. You want me to warm you up some of that barbecue from last night?" Nathan asked.

"Yea big bwudda," Enos said, trying to sit still.

"Boy, you better stop trying to lie to me too."

"O'tay I torry."

Nathan sloppily mopped up the mess of lemonade on the floor. Without ensuring that the floor wasn't sticky, he turned hi attention to the barbecue. He put a piece of steak, rib and chicken in the microwave for them to eat and set the cook time to three minutes. After that, he poured them both a glass of lemonade, then took the lemonade to the table and sat next to Enos. Even he paid no attention to the obvious, finger marks in the cake in the fridge.

"Where Punkin at?" Nathan asked.

"Updairs asweep," Enos told him.

"I thought you was him in here until something told me to get up and look. How long you been up?"

"I'on know."

The microwave beeped, so Nathan stood up, took the food out, grabbed a plate for Enos, and put two pieces of ribs and a piece of chicken on it. They sat down and ate. To Nathan's surprise, he saw Enos was really hungry, 'cause he ate all of his food and still wanted more, when, usually, he didn't eat much. So, Nathan went and put another piece of rib and chicken on his plate and warmed it up for him.

Once they finished, Nathan took Enos upstairs, gave him a bath and put Enos in some clean clothes. By this time, Punkin had awakened and he could smell the aroma of barbecue. So, he headed straight downstairs to the kitchen, but before he got to the kitchen, he saw Enos and Nathan sitting in the living room watching cartoons.

"Dair he go big bwudda." Enos said, pointing to Punkin coming down the steps.

"What about me?" Punkin asked.

"I'on know. Big bwudda jus' acks wur ou was."

"Oh. Wassup big bruh? I smell food."

"Wassup? I just warmed up some leftovers from last night in the microwave." Nathan told him.

"Ok, I'm about to warm me up some now." Punkin told them.

A few minutes later, Punkin had returned with a piece of ribs, chicken and steak on his plate. He still had the munchies from smoking weed the night before. As he was eating his food, their big sister, Sheila, came downstairs, "Damn that shit smells good. Woke me up out of a deep sleep," Sheila said.

That's when she spotted Punkin eating.

"Come here boy and let me taste that." She said walking over to his plate breaking her a piece of chicken and steak. Then she went on into the kitchen and fixed her own.

"Hey Nathan and Enos."

"Eey big susta." Enos said.

"Hey cry baby." Nathan said, teasing her about last night.

"Go to hell, Nathan." She said with a smile and went on into the kitchen.

"Mama gonna kill us if we don't save her some." Nathan said.

"Well, mama better hurry up and get up. Shit, it's a bunch of that stuff in there left over from last night anyway." Sheila told him.

"Big sister, when mama get up, I'ma ask her can we spend our money today. If she say yeah, will you and Nathan take us shoppin'?" Punkin asked, without having any idea that Sheila didn't know anything about the money his mama had given them.

"What money, boy? And you can't go shopping with no five and ten dollars," she said.

"We got more than that! She gave me and Enos $250.00 apiece. But she gave Nathan and Samantha a whole lot of money," Punkin told her.

"When was this?" Sheila asked Punkin, while looking at Nathan with an evil eye.

Sheila knew Punkin was unaware of what he was doing and was going to tell her everything.

"I don't know, ask Nathan."

"When was this Mr. Nathan?" Sheila asked.

"Boy, you talk to damn much," Nathan said, looking at Punkin.

"Leave him alone nigga, he didn't know. Now answer my question," Sheila persisted.

"I don't know, hell about a week or two ago, som'n like that."

"How much Mama gave you and Samantha?" Sheila continued her interrogation.

"None of your business, girl. You wanna know, ask Mama." Samantha diverted.

"Oh, I am, as soon as she wake her lil ass up. How she gonna give y'all some money and don't give me some too. Hell." Sheila complained, feeling intentionally left out.

"Cause it's my money, and I do what the hell I wanna do with it. And you sho ain't gotta wait any longer sister gal, 'cause I'm right damn here. I been up here the whole time listening to yo' ass. So, ask away," Cha-Cha said, coming down the stairs and was now standing at the bottom eyeing Sheila.

When Sheila realized she was exposed, she put her hand over her mouth with surprised eyes so wide, she looked like a deer in headlights.

"Don't be looking damn crazy now! Here I go, so you can question me, since you had all kinds of damn questions and interrogations a minute ago. Now yo' prosecutin' ass silent as a church mouse. Come on prosecutor, don't let the cat swallow your tongue now."

"I didn't mean it like that, Mama."

"I know goddamn well you didn't."

Nathan was looking at Sheila, with a smirk on his face, because just a minute ago, she was all hard and bad. But since Mama showed up and caught her, she was copping deuces.

"I'm just saying Mama. Why I ain't got no money being as I'm one of your children too. I ain't never did nothing wrong to you." Sheila said, reversing her role, now pleading her case.

"Y'all goin to take them shopping today like that boy ask y'all to?" Cha-Cha asked her.

"You know we is. Well I am, I don't know about Mr. Nathan right here."

"You can stop trying to throw me under the bus, girl, 'cause Mama already know I'm gonna do it. Oh yeah, I already fed and bathed Enos too," Nathan retaliated sticking out his tongue at Sheila.

"Ok baby. Punkin, go on upstairs and take you a bath and get ready to go," Cha-Cha said as she continued on to the kitchen.

"Nathan! Come here!" she yelled from the kitchen.

"Yes ma'am," Nathan said as he got up and went into the kitchen.

"Go upstairs and grab that money outta the side table next to my bed."

"Yes ma'am." Then he turned and left.

He returned a minute later handing her the money.

"Why my floor so sticky, and why do it look like Enos finger prints in my cake?" she asked.

"I caught 'em in here this morning eatin' it and making a mess of himself and the floor with wasted lemonade...I tried to clean it all up...Guess I didn't do too good of a job.... I didn't notice the fingerprints. Just tried to get'm something to eat."

"I see, said the blind man." Cha-Cha accepted.

She went to the counter and counted out $2,000.00. She was going to give Sheila one for herself and the other one for Punkin and Enos to go shopping wit.

Sheila walked in the kitchen and started smiling when she laid eyes on the money.

"Here girl, here's $2,000.00. One is for you and the other one is for them to go shopping wit.

"Mama, them boys ain't go'n need no $1,000.00 to shop wit."

"Well it's my money, and get 'em whatever they want. Whatever they don't use, brang it back, and I'll put it back up for'em."

"Yes ma'am. Thank you, Mama." Sheila said huggin and kissin her Mama on the cheek.

Sheila then went upstairs to get ready to go and made sure both of her lil brothers was ready so they could leave. After an hour and a half they was headed to the bus stop, so they could go downtown to 5 Points Mall to shop.

"Nathan, go and clean that mop out in the bathroom, and bring me the mop bucket with some Lysol in hot water, and I'm go'n teach you how to mop up a mess," instructed Cha-Cha.

Chapter 23

Cha-Cha was upstairs in her bedroom with her husband as he was getting ready to go out somewhere when he asked her the whereabouts of Punkin and Enos. She told him Nathan and Sheila had taken them shopping. She then drifted to thinking about how much time she had left before Tyrone made it back in town, which was almost two weeks. So, she thought she'd go ahead and grab the other twelve pounds today and sell'em.

"Where you about to go?" Cha-Cha asked Droup.

"Hell, probably to see a man about a mule, why?"

"Don't be getting smart with me, bastard. 'Cause I might need you to take me down to Samantha's apartment so I can pick up my reefer," she told him.

"Ok, well tell me what time you want to go, and we'll make it happen, captain."

"Now that sounds more like it. Let me call her first," Cha-Cha said.

Cha-Cha picked up the phone and called Samantha.

"She didn't answer. Let me try her again," Cha-Cha told Droup.

She called back and Samantha answered on the first ring.

"Hello?"

"Why you didn't answer the first time I called?" Cha-Cha asked her.

"I was in the bathroom, Mama. I can't just sit by the phone 24/7 waiting for you to call. I do have a life myself, you know," Samantha told her.

"Yeah, and it revolves around me," Cha-Cha responded jokingly.

"Not no more, lil girl. But wassup, Mama? You must want to come get the rest of that weed."

"My baby is growing up. And how you know? Me and your daddy will be down there in a lil while to get twelve of'em. I'm going to keep one for myself. Plus, I ain't got nothin but two more weeks until Tyrone comes back into town anyway," Cha-Cha told her.

"Ok, Mama. I will be here."

"Bye, baby."

As soon as Cha-Cha got dressed to leave, the phone started ringing with her customers calling, looking for some weed. She told them it would be another week, just to see their reactions. Just like always, she got the reaction she wanted. They were desperate for the reefer, and she knew she wouldn't drag it out for a full week, rather three or four more days at most.

After about thirty minutes, they were able to go pick up the reefer. When they got to Samantha's apartment, they were surprised to see the door wide open and hear loud music coming from her apartment. They just looked at each other and parked and got out. They also noticed seven kids out in the front yard playing and three women sitting on her front porch. As Cha-Cha and Droup approached the front door, they were met by a smiling Samantha.

"Hey y'all this is my mama and daddy," Samantha told the three women on the front porch.

"Hey, my name is Pam," one girl said.

"Hey, I'm Janice," another one said.

"Hello, and I'm Alice," the last girl added.

"Hey, how y'all doing? I'm Cha-Cha, and this is my husband, Droup."

"Wassup now?" Droup said.

Cha-Cha looked and saw a pack of rolling papers sitting on the ground next to one of the girls on the porch.

"Did you put my meat in the cooler, like I asked you to?" Cha-Cha asked Samantha privately.

"No ma'am, but come on, and we can do it now," Samantha told her.

All three of them went inside to grab the reefer. Samantha closed the door, but nobody was curious enough to pay any attention to that. Two minutes later, the door opened and the three girls were unmoved, still lounging on the porch. Cha-Cha, Droup, and Samantha all went back outside. Droup took the cooler to the car and grabbed himself a beer.

"Y'all smoke weed?" Cha-Cha asked the three women on the front porch.

"Yes, ma'am, we do," Janice told her.

Cha-Cha reached down in her bra and grabbed her cigarette pack. She pulled out one Tie Stick and passed it to one of the girls, winking at Samantha.

"Here, light this up," Cha-Cha told the girl.

Janice reached for the joint, and fired it up. Soon as she inhaled, she choked until she almost threw up. Everyone else was looking at her, then she finally passed it to the other two, and they did the same thing. Cha-Cha got it, hit it, and choked, but not as bad as the others since she was getting the hang of it. The other three had tears running down their cheeks, and were already high as hell off just one hit.

"What the hell type reefer is that, Ms. Cha-Cha?" Janice asked.

"Yeah, 'cause I ain't never smoked nothin' like it," Pam added.

"Yeah, please let us know, because I'm high as hell off just one hit," Alice told Cha-Cha.

"This right here is called Tie Stick, and it's the best shit around," Cha-Cha told all three.

"We been hearing about this reefer, but was never about to get none. They say it cost like hell, too," Pam said.

"Yeah, it used to be $10 a joint, but now since it's a drought, they chargin' 15 and sometimes 20. All depends on who you know," Cha-Cha told them.

"For a joint?" Janice asked.

"Yeah, baby and it's worth it too. Y'all will see. I bet y'all don't smoke any more reefer for another 5 to 6 hours," Cha-Cha said.

"Are you serious? Off just one hit?" Janice said, not believing it.

"Serious as a heart attack," Cha-Cha told her.

"If that's the truth, and you know where to get it from, I'm about to put every reefer man out here outta business," Janice said.

"I know that's right girl. I am wit' you," Pam told her.

"Me too," Alice signed on, finally able to talk.

"They want $350 for an ounce right now, though. But if you're selling nothin but joints, you'll make anywhere from $750 to $1000 easy off joints alone. Not even including what y'all smoke out of it. Here. Y'all keep the rest of this joint. My daughter has my number and will let me know when y'all ready," Cha-Cha told them.

"Ok, thank you. We will," Janice told her.

As Cha-Cha and Droup were getting ready to leave, the neighborhood ice cream truck came around, and all seven kids ran up to their mommas, asking for ice cream. All the moms responded, "I ain't got no money." Samantha looked at her mama and knew what she was about to do.

"All these y'all kids," Cha-Cha asked.

"Yes, ma'am," Alice told her.

"Ok," Cha-Cha said, looking at the kids, "all y'all come wit me. Let's go get some ice cream," she told them.

All seven kids ran to the ice cream truck. When they got to the truck, Cha-Cha told the driver, "Give these kids whatever they want."

Then she told the kids, "Get whatever y'all want."

"Yaaaay! Thank you Miss...Miss.....", one of the kids attempted.

"Cha-Cha...I'm Cha-Cha." The little lady said, introducing herself.

"Thank you Miss Cha-Cha", the kids almost said in unison, and giggled.

"Y'all welcome kids", responded Cha-Cha

The kids got whatever they wanted and were so excited! They got ice cream, soda pops, popsicles, candy, chips, and whatever else they could carry. This was a great day for them to play.

Screaming out of joy, they all went as quickly as they could back to the yard with their ice cream, other goodies, and a smile. Cha-Cha walked back to the porch feeling good about herself, happy that she could make a difference for the moms and the kids. All the women started saying "Thank you" as she approached with surprising looks on their faces..

"Just glad I could help out....Y'all welcome", Cha-Cha stated modestly.

Then Droup asked the women if they drank beer, and Alice responded, "Yes sir."

Droup went to the trunk and brought them a cold six-pack of beer. Then Cha-Cha and Droup said their goodbyes and left.

"Why you give them that beer?" Cha-Cha asked him.

"So, they would think that was what was in the cooler," he told her.

"Smart thinking!....but didn't I ask Samantha if she had packed meat in the cooler when we first got there???"

"Yea...that...I knowww! But you can never be too careful", Droup dodged.

The phone was ringing as they walked in the door. Cha-Cha walked in the kitchen and picked it up while Droup headed upstairs with the cooler.

"Hello?" Cha-Cha said.

"Hey, it's Tyrone."

"Wassup sugga, tell me something good"

"Well, I'll be back in a week, and I'll have something special for my favorite girl."

"Ok, I sho can't wait. I'm just about out of food too. I only got twelve packs of meat left, and I'm about to start cooking on them now or tomorrow."

"I'll restock the freezer when I get home. You won't go hungry. I promise."

"Ok," Cha-Cha responded.

"Bye, now" Tyrone said.

"Bye sugga."

Cha-Cha hung up, smiling from ear to ear, because, next week, she would have no less than a hundred pounds, and instead of selling ounces, she would go ahead and start selling nothing but pounds. She thought that by her buying so much of it, she should be able to get'em discounted between $600 to $800 a pound. She would let them go for $2,500 a pound or even $2,000 a pound which would still be a good profit.

Instead of waiting for days, she would have Nathan and Charlie help her, and she would start selling it tomorrow. As soon as Nathan came back from taking Punkin and Enos shopping, they would start breaking down the reefer. She called one of Charlie's girls and gave word to have him come over to the apartment. Then she went upstairs to find the pounds already stacked up on the bed with the scale and the bags too. Cha-Cha just looked at her husband, who was grinning like a chess cat.

"What you think you doing?" she asked him.

"'Bout to sell me some reefer. What it look like?"

"You don't know nothing about selling no reefer!" she reminded him.

"I might not, but hell, I'ma learn today. Come on let's go!" he told her.

"Are you serious?" Cha-Cha asked him.

"Hell yeah, I'm serious. Come on!"

So, they started breaking it down and weighing it up. She showed her husband how to work the scale, making sure all the ounces were spot on 28 grams. She also showed him how to roll it up and put it into bags. She told him to make sure it was put back into the foil too. They were still working a few hours later when Sheila came back from shopping with Nathan, Punkin, and Enos. When they got back from shopping, they could smell the reefer, so they headed upstairs. When they opened the door to their mama's room and saw their daddy helping, all movement came to a screeching halt.

"Daddy, what you doing?!!" a shocked Sheila asked him.

"What it look like?" he replied.

Nathan was speechless.

"Oh, lord. I know this family is turning into a cartel now. You got my Daddy in here bagging up reefer. Look, he got the scale and everything!" Sheila said, unable to believe what she was seeing.

Punkin immediately ran over to the bed, and said "I wanna help!"

Enos was right behind him and added, "Me too!"

Their daddy was about to say something, but his wife cut him off before he could even get a word out.

"Don't you dare say a word to them. Hell, look at *you,*" she then went to explaining to her babies what to do. Sheila and Nathan just stood and watched.

"Ok, I'm going to break down the reefer, and y'all daddy is going to weigh it up. Punkin, you are going to put them in bags and wrap them in the aluminum foil, and then pass them to Enos. Enos, I want you to stack them in the cooler on the floor," she instructed.

Nathan went around to the side of the bed where Punkin was, to show him how to properly wrap them up in aluminum foil. Sheila was on the phone by then, calling Samantha and telling her what was going on. Then she called Baby Girl and told her. None of them could believe their daddy was actually helping with breaking down the reefer.

Samantha said it best, "Money has corrupted our family."

"Yeah, you right, but, at least, it's in the family," Sheila said and hung up.

They continued to work until all 162 ounces were done.

Afterwards, Punkin and Enos showed everyone the clothes and shoes they bought. They spent almost $800 on their stuff. There were so many bags, they had to take a taxi cab back home instead of the bus. Sheila gave her mom the change that was left over from the shopping and went downstairs to fix herself something to eat.

Cha-Cha was now putting out the word that she had found some more ounces for sale, but the dude who had them wanted $450 apiece for them. She said he didn't really want to sell them, but if he did, it would have to be at that price. She told her customers she had to do it that way to meet her mark. Everyone said ok and that they would be there in the morning to pick up the same 24 ounces as last time. She was looking at making $72,900 after she had sold the last ounce. One-hundred twenty of them were already gone, and she would only have 42 left to sell around Atlanta for the same price this time.

"Nathan, you know you can't go nowhere tonight, right?" Cha-Cha said.

"Naw, I didn't. Why not?" Nathan asked.

"You see all this damn reefer? But, I mean, most of it will be gone in the morning before 11am. I'm about to call Samantha now, so she can rent a car tonight and be over here early. I called Charlie, but he ain't shown up yet," she told him.

Cha-Cha picked up the phone and called Samantha.

"Hello?" Samantha answered.

"Hey, baby. What you doing?" Cha-Cha asked.

"Nothing, just sitting in the apartment chillin," Samantha told her.

"Ok, I need you to rent another car, and do the same thing as last time," Cha-Cha told her.

"Yes, ma'am. I will see you at two."

"Ok, baby. Bye"

"Bye, Mama."

Chapter 24

The next morning Cha-Cha's phone started ringing at 8:30AM. From there, it just kept ringing back to back, one call after another. The first person who called was Pete, to see if she was ready for him to come over. To her surprise, Charlie was at the apartment when she woke up at 7:29 AM. Since everything and everybody was in place, she told Pete and the rest of'em to come on. All five of her out of town customers showed up like clockwork. They never complained and were never late. If anything, they'd show up early, and the money was nearly always on point. She was upstairs when the knock came at the door from Pete.

Knock! Knock! Knock!

"Who is it?" she said from the upstairs window over the front porch.

"Me, Pete."

"Ok, hold on, I'm on my way down now."

A few seconds later, she opened the door to let him in, and they both went into the living room. He reached inside his jacket and pulled out a bag with $10,800.00 in it and handed it to her. Then she told him," Have a seat, and I'll be right back.

Cha-Cha then turned and went into the kitchen, opened the refrigerator, and returned with a small paper bag with 24 ounces in it. She gave it to Pete, then she walked him back to the front and let him out. As soon as he was walking to his car, she saw everyone else pulling up within five seconds of each other. When she saw that, she didn't even attempt to close the door, she just stood there waiting for all of'em to come in. First, Jerome came and hugged her at the door, he was followed by Ted, James and Joe. After they all were in the living room seated, she closed the door and went to join them.

"Damn, I sho didn't expect for y'all to be here so fast and early like this," she said.

"Shit, if I was to wait any longer, I feel I might miss out," Joe said.

"Hell, me too," Ted said.

"And I damn sho can't afford to take that chance," James said.

"See how you got all of us by the balls Cha-Cha," Jerome said.

"Hell, this bastard got all of us by the 'balls.' Not just y'all, me too." Everybody started laughing. "One thang all of y'all can bet y'all money on… If I tell anyone of y'all I got something for y'all, it's going to be here until y'all come and get it," Cha-Cha reassured them.

"Well, that I can say is truth, 'cause you never let me down," Joe said.

"Me either." Jerome said.

"From day one, you been good to me." Ted said.

"You show didn't see me complaining." James said.

"I'm sho glad y'all feel that way, and I'ma continue to do my best and keep y'all satisfied," Cha-Cha said.

With that, she got up, went into the kitchen, opened the refrigerator, and came back with four brown paper bags. She handed each of them a bag. They then gave her the money and left after giving her a quick hug and a 'thank you.' After they left, Cha-Cha locked her front door. She went to the steps to find Nathan standing at the top with his Uzi in his hand. She just looked and went into the bedroom where she dropped five paper sacks of money on the bed. Each bag contained $10,800.00 a piece: that added up to $54,000.00 that she'd made in 20 minutes.

"Come on y'all, help me count this! It should be $54,000.00 in all. Grab a bag."

She gave one to Samantha, Charlie and Nathan. Plus, she took one herself. They all counted the money, and it was exactly the right amount. They all counted the last one together. When it all added up, she took another $1,000.00 from her personal money and put it with the 54 stacks to make it $55,000.00 in total. She would put it with her $170,000.00 she already had put up to give her $225,000.00 in all put up, not to mention anticipated profit from the other 42 ounces she had left to sell. That would bring her another $18,900.00 for her to be able to spend freely. She now had over $200,000.00 put away. She just needed Tyrone to get back in the mix.

"Mama, how you do it? You make it look so easy," Samantha said,

"Hard work and dedication, baby, is all I can say. Knowing when your break has come and taking advantage of every opportunity when it comes your way. Look, go ahead and take that money and put it up with the rest. I'ma give you some money later on when I get rid of these other 42 ounces."

"Yes ma'am."

"Nathan and Charlie, I think she can handle this one by herself. I want y'all to stay here with me, 'cause we 'bout to start planning for this shipment. Call me when you get home, Samantha."

"Ok Mama, I will."

Samantha got up, went out the back door, and locked it back with her key. She then headed home to put the money up. After she was gone, Cha-Cha started talking to Nathan and Charlie.

"Tyrone should be back next week. I thought it was going to be two more weeks, but he called me yesterday and told me he'd be back a week early. So that's why I decided to go ahead and sell the rest of that reefer I had. I feel this next load I get from'm, I'll let y'all sell ounces while I sell pounds. Remember, he just sold me thirty pounds for $20,000, so I'm guessing I should be able to buy a hundred pounds anywhere from $60,000 to $70,000. On the low end, I could sell each pound for $1,500 to $2,000.00 and still make a nice profit."

"The way this shit here just moved, they'll be glad to pay that for a pound, maybe more, 'cause I'm thinkin' $2500 a pound, really." Nathan said.

"Hell yeah shawty! You was just selling them ounces for $350.00 then jumped'em up to $450.00 and still didn't have any complaints. So just imagine how these niggas gonna act now," Charlie said.

While Charlie was talking, the phone started ringing, and she picked it up.

"Hello?"

"Mama, I'm at home."

"Ok baby."

"This gives you $225,000.00 put up down here, right?"

"Yeah, that's right."

"Ok Mama just makin sure," Samantha said.

"I know you got your mama, baby. That's why I trust you so much," Cha-Cha told her.

"I know Mama."

"I should be calling you later on to come and get you some money."

"Mama! I ain't worried about no money. Talk to you later."

"Ok bye."

"Bye."

One week later, Cha-Cha was in the bathroom, and her husband was in the bedroom watching the news. She heard him call her name with urgency in his voice, "Cha-Cha, come here, hurry up!!!!"

She ran out of the bathroom from washing her face. When she saw what was on the TV screen, it broke her heart.

"Ain't that's your boy, Tyrone, right there?"

"What the fuck!!!! Turn it up." Cha-Cha told him.

"It's coming up after the next commercial!" After a few minutes passed, he said, "Here it is."

"This is Channel 2 Action News. BREAKING NEWS! Today F.B.I agents finally caught one of the ring leaders in one of the largest drug rings in American history. Today they stormed the house of Mr. Tyrone Fernandez. This morning around 7:30 AM, agents seized over 3 million dollars in cash, over 10,000 pounds of marijuana and an arsenal of firearms ranging from assault rifles and hand guns to RPG's and Uzi's. Agents also say Mr. Fernandez had over fifteen mansions in three different countries with five of them here in the U.S.. Mr. Fernandez was running drugs in thirty of the fifty states in America. The F.B.I. has been watching him for the last five to ten years, but say he's been pushing drugs for at least twenty-five. They estimate him to have made anywhere from half a billion to a billion dollars. Agents are expecting that lawyers, doctors, judges, senators and plenty more powerful people are on his pay roll.

When Cha-Cha saw and heard all that, she could've sworn she was in a very bad dream until her husband snapped her out of it and back to a grim reality.

"Cha-Cha, you need to get everything outta this goddamn apartment, everything from down at Samantha's apartment, and put it all somewhere safe. 'Cause hell, if they've been watching him that long, and you've been dealing with him, then they might be watching you too."

"Come on grab that scale and them bags, so we can get it out of here. We ain't goin to call Samantha, we'll just go down there 'cause you might be right."

They got everything out of the apartment, put it in the car, and drove to Samantha's apartment. When they pulled up, Samantha looked surprised, because usually her mama would've called first before she came. She knew something was wrong as soon as they got out of the car. They all stepped inside and closed the door.

"What's wrong?" Samantha asked, concerned.

"Tyrone got busted this morning by the Feds, and the news says they've been watching him for years. So, we just need to get all of this money and that last pound of reefer outta the apartment, and bury it," Cha-Cha told her.

Samantha went and got the big cooler. She went to her stove, opened the bottom, pulled it out, and started stacking the money in the cooler. They would take it over to Cha-Cha's daddy's house, bury it in his back yard that night, and bury the pound somewhere else. When they had all the money together, they took everything out of the apartment and headed to Cha-Cha's daddy's house.

"Samantha, get that pound outta here too."

"What you want me to do with it, Mama?"

"Go to the pay phone, call JJ, and have him meet you somewhere. Give it to'm, and tell'm I said I'll call him later on tonight," Cha-Cha told her.

"Ok"

On her way over to her daddy's house, Cha-Cha stopped by a pay phone, called him and told him she was on her way over there and that she needed him to hold something for her. Then she got back into the car, and they headed on over to his house. He was sitting outside playing checkers in his front yard with one of his friends. He raised his head from his checkers game and looked at him when they pulled up. He got up from his game and headed in the house when he saw them get outta the car.

"Daddy, I need to bury some money in your back yard," Cha-Cha told him.

"In my yard. For what?" her father, Sam Sparks, asked.

"My people got busted by the Feds this morning. I didn't have no idea that he was as big as he was. So, since I been dealing with him for a while now, I'm thinking they might be watching me, too,"

"Don't tell me that dude I just seen on the news with that funny name is who you talkin' about. The one they caught with all that money, reefer, and guns. What's his name, Her..Hernandez, or som'n like that?"

"Yea that's him, FERnandez, Tyrone Fernandez."

"How much money is it?"

This was the question she dreaded, but knew it was coming.

"It's $225,000, Daddy."

He sat up and his eyes got big, real big, as if he was afraid that he had heard her right.

"Say that again? Cause I know I ain't heard that right."

"Yeah, Daddy you heard me right. It's $225,000. But you don't have to worry, I'll pay you for doing this for me."

"200 Twenty Fiiiive dol....is you kiddin' me? I don't know, Cha-Cha...I mean it's mighty funny you wanna run over here now, when you need my help but ain't came to check on me to see if I needed anything, nothing, even though I didn't. But it's just the principle, Cha-Cha."

"I know it's been a while, Daddy, but you know I was coming to see you. Plus, I wanted to do something special for you. And knowing you, you wouldn't have taken the money or help from me anyway.

"At least you know me. Go on out there and bury your money while you still got time." Sam authorized.

"Droup, go get the money," ordered Cha-Cha.

Her husband went outside and got the cooler out of the back seat of the car. He went back into the living room where they were and sat the cooler on the floor in front of his wife. Cha-Cha opened the cooler and counted out $25,000 and gave it to her daddy, while Droup went outside by himself to bury the rest.

"Daddy this is $25,000, and $5,000 of it is yours. Put the other $20,000 up in this house just in case I need it for a lawyer or bond. Hopefully, I won't need it though."

"Ok look Cha-Cha, you're grown, and you goin' to do what you wanna do, but you need to get outta that shit before it's too late and you end up in prison for the rest of your life. Do you want to be away from them kids of yours? Don't you think you got enough money to go legit? At least think about it. I know you're going to be hard-headed just like you've been your whole life."

"Yessir, Daddy. You're right, I do, and I will think about it."

"Alright...now, go on back and help that damn man. He works hard enough as it is."

With that said, she got up and went out back to help her husband, who was out there digging a hole big enough for the cooler. He just looked up with sweat on his face as his wife walked out and grabbed a shovel and started helping him dig.

In forty-five minutes, they had dug the hole, wrapped the money, and buried the cooler in the back yard. The good thing about her burying the money in her daddy's back yard was that the yard was shielded by two 15-foot-high wooden fences, so nobody could look in or get in his yard.

When they had finished burying the money, they both went inside, washed up, and headed out the front door. She kissed and hugged her daddy, who never even looked up from the checkers game he had resumed. He did shake her husband's hand though. Then, they got in the car and left.

"Damn!" Cha-Cha said.

"What now?" Droup asked.

"We still got this damn scale and these bags in the car," Cha-Cha reminded him.

"Hell, throw that shit out the window! You can always buy a scale and bags."

He pulled over at the liquor store, and she reached in the back seat, got the items and threw them in the dumpster. She got back in the car, and they drove off."

"You know I still got most of that $5,000 you gave me," Droup told her.

"Naw, I didn't know. But that's your money, plus I still got about like $11,000 put up myself, where I can get to it just in case I need it."

"You just full of surprises ain't you?" Droup commented.

"Your wife ain't got this far by being stupid, baby," Cha-Cha reminded him.

"Yea I know."

They pulled back up in front of their apartment. They got out, went inside, and went upstairs. Once they were upstairs, Cha-Cha just sat on the bed and went all the way silent. Droup knew what was wrong with her. He knew she was thinking about Tyrone and how everything seemed like it just caved in her face. But she had to snap out of it, because the Feds weren't anything to play with---point blank period.

"Look Cha-Cha, I know that what just happened to you got you worried and all, but the Feds ain't nothing to play with, period. You don't need to touch any type of illegal shit or that money for at least a year. Now, you can be hard-headed and do whatever you want, but you got enough money put up, and, plus, together we got $15,000 right now. Hell, we know how to live like we po', but we ain't really po' as some people. You need to listen to me," Droup told her.

"I hear you," she responded.

"A'ight goddammit, I see now you gonna be hard-headed and go to the chain gang."

"I said I hear you goddammit!" Cha-Cha responded, getting irritated.

Droup didn't say another word. He just looked at her and shook his head, because he knew she wasn't going to listen.

Chapter 25

Nathan, Punkin, Charlie and Enos all came in the apartment together. They had been out all day at the Omni, downtown, watching movies and playing video games at The Gold Mine. Soon as they all got upstairs, Nathan was the first to notice the look on their mama's face. She was sitting on the bed looking like she'd lost her mama all over again.

"What's wrong with you, Mama?" Nathan said.

"Yeah, shawty. Wassup? Why you lookin like that?" Charlie asked.

"I bet Smooth done stole her money again," Punkin said angrily.

"The Feds got Tyrone this morning, with so much shit, I doubt if he'll ever see the streets again. They say he was one of the biggest drug dealers in American history," she explained, but was cut off by her husband.

"Here it is, right here," Droup said.

As the Channel 2 News showed the coverage of Tyrone again, they all listened, and heard the news repeat the same information about Tyrone. Nathan and Charlie couldn't believe what they were hearing. To think that Tyrone had been right there in their apartment, growing fond of their mama. She had the plug of the 80's. Plugs like that were very hard to come by and she had it. Now they could see why she was so hurt and upset. But, at least, she was still at home with them and not with the Feds. After the news was over, Nathan just whistled.

"Why you say that?" Cha-Cha said.

"Because remember when we were downstairs in the living room… What he had said about putting all your eggs in one basket?"

"Yeah, I do remember," Cha-Cha said.

"So now do you still think that was all he had?" Nathan asked.

"Hell naw, probably just a flex package for him," Cha-Cha replied.

"My point exactly. But damn what you gonna do now?"

"Hell, she better do like I told her and don't do shit. Them damn Feds ain't nothin' to play wit now ," Droup said.

"Man, shut the hell up!" Cha-Cha said.

"You know what, you can do whatever the hell you wanna goddamn do. I ain't got time for this shit!" Droup got up and walked out of the room, went downstairs, and walked out the front door. Then he got in the car and drove off.

"He's right mama! I know you might not wanna hear it, but he is." Nathan said.

"I know he is. But dammit, this shit just fucked me over. I don't know what the fuck to do right now," Cha-Cha told them.

"It ain't like you're broke and hurting for nothing, shawty." Charlie said.

"I know. I made sure I got everything outta here today too: bags, scale and all. All I got left here is a lil money I made off them last ounces. I also went and got everything from down at Samantha's apartment too. I sent JJ that last pound for him to put up for me. Charlie, I want you to call him and let him know what's goin on. Find a pay phone though, 'cause I'm not trusting my phone at all."

"Ok" Charlie said.

Soon as she said that, the phone rang.

"Hello?"

"Hey, baby this JJ what you......" Before he could finish she cut him off.

"Hold on, don't say nothing. Home boy will call you and let you know what's goin on."

He caught on asap.

"Who, Mechanicsville, shawty?" JJ asked.

"Yea."

"Ok Mama, bye," JJ said.

"Bye baby."

"That was JJ right there, so, Charlie, he's waiting on your call. Go handle that for me."

"You know I got you, shawty." Charlie said.

"For now, I'm just gonna lay low for a while. For how long, I can't say. But as of right now, I'm chillin."

"Well, we'd rather have you home and broke than to not have you at home at all, Mama." Nathan said.

"Well, I still got my cigarette pack full of my personals, and it should last for a while. Here, light this up Charlie." She said, handing Charlie a joint to light up.

"Mama, what you ever do with all that other weed you had that time when I was helping you bag it up?" Punkin asked.

Everyone in the room looked puzzled, 'cause they was wondering what he was talking about. But she knew he was talkin bout them five pounds from the first time she let him help her.

"I don't know whatever happened to that weed, 'cause I sho don't remember selling it," she told the group.

Then it struck her. One day when she was going up in her stash spot in Punkin's room, something brushed her hand, but she paid it no attention. But she didn't remember ever putting it in there, not unless she'd done it one day when she was extremely high and forgot about it. She got up and went in Punkin's room, closed the door, got on her crate, and checked the spot. She felt a bag and pulled it down. She looked inside of it and those same five pounds was sitting in the bag. She put 'em right back up there, where she would leave them for hard times. Her baby, Punkin, had saved the day. She went into the room and said she had to think about it, because she couldn't remember. But one thing she did know, reefer got better with time. So, the longer it sat up there, the more it matured, and it had at least three months on it already.

When Droup left the apartment, he was mad as hell, because he knew his wife wasn't going to listen to him. So, he went to the liquor store and bought himself a half pint of liquor and a six pack of beer, then he rode around trying to clear his head. He loved his wife, there was no question about it, but she was just so damn stubborn. If she was going to start back selling drugs, and he found out, he didn't know what he would do. But one thing for sure, he didn't want that shit around him or his kids. He rode around for a few more hours and went back home with his mind made up with his own lil secret. He went in the apartment, went straight upstairs, and got in the bed.

"Where the hell you been?" Cha-Cha asked him.

"Don't worry 'bout where the hell I been." Droup said and went to sleep.

Then the phone rang.

"Hello?" Cha-Cha answered.

"Shawty, I'm glad you're still up, 'cause I need to talk to you. I'm on my way back right now." Charlie said.

Ten minutes later Charlie was coming in through the door.

"Shawty, I spotted them folks in the woods over by Price, so they gotta be watchin you! So, you need to chill out. Ok" Charlie told her.

"You sure?" Cha-Cha asked him.

"I'm positive," Charlie told her.

"Ok, hold on, I'll be right back," Cha-Cha told him.

After a few minutes she returned with the five pounds of reefer from Punkin's closet, gave them to Charlie, and sent him out the back door.

The walls seemed to be closing in on her. What would she do? What could she do?

The End

Yunus Abdul Wahid